CLACKAMAS LITERARY REVIEW

2023
Volume XXVII

Clackamas Community College
Oregon City, Oregon

CLACKAMAS LITERARY REVIEW

Managing Editor
Matthew Warren

Associate Editors
Jennifer Davis   Amy Warren

Christopher Zimmerly-Beck

Assistant Editors & Designers
Emma Bellafronto   Silvia Diaz Diaz   Rosalyn Fullington

Shawn Schenck   Zelda Merlin Stroup

Cover Art
Old Bridge and Birch Trees by Tessa Broadie

The Clackamas Literary Review is published annually at Clackamas Community College. Manuscripts are read from September 1st to December 31st. By submitting your work to *CLR*, you indicate your consent for us to publish accepted work in print and online. Issues I–XI are available through our website; issues XII–XXVI are available on our Submittable, and through your favorite online bookseller.

Clackamas Literary Review
19600 Molalla Avenue, Oregon City, Oregon 97045
ISBN: 978-1-7320333-5-1
Printed by Lightning Source
www.clackamasliteraryreview.org

CONTENTS

EDITORS' NOTE

POETRY

PROSE

Editors' Note

We are the sum of our experiences. Everything we do, everything that is done to us, leaves impressions—sometimes light markings, sometimes deep scars—which never go away. We can try to hide them from others—and sometimes, we can—but we can never hide them from ourselves. To try to forget is to reject a part of who we are, leaving us less whole.

These impressions, for better or worse, become a part of us, a part of who we are as people. To live is to accept what scars us. As we emerge into the world, unabashed and unashamed, we must take a look inside—face our memories, our pain, our joy, our traumas, our triumphs, and come to understand who we are. With this perspective, we are able to put to page a facsimile of ourselves, a work as unique as the living, breathing person who created it.

We here at the *Clackamas Literary Review* have worked to gather a collection of these facsimiles. Care to have a look?

Signs

Diane Averill

When the mist begins a slow spin
around the pines

look for the shimmer of a minnow
just after it has disappeared from the skies

and if you forget to see
these things we once shared

then you might notice when your shadow
disappears gradually into the night with mine

or maybe when your singing mind
slows down into soft sleep

you may begin to know
I'll be visiting tonight in a space between your dreams

and we'll continue the conversation
we never really left.

A Few Suggestions (from a Hill)

Evan Litsios

Be slow, be kind
make like a small animal
frequent an area in the woods
become familiar with its features
start big, go small
return often

Go after a rain
when drips and drops mask
the silence and the wind
the twigs that fill the space
and slowly go
pad along in your fur
sniff and twitch suddenly
hold your gaze
be brave
let that thing creep up
and show you what it is

There are paths
on the forest floor
follow them

A Few Suggestions (from a Hill)

stop every few steps
there are trees without
leaves around their bases
as though many priests
have walked around them
or princes calling up
to let down some golden gift
or squirrels
going about their business

Let it shrink around you
allow the moss to take all
the time   it needs
above the clouds, the bronze gong
confirms you can walk
a little longer
before dark

Boy

Andrew Robin

I've reached that part
in *The Red Pony* by
John Steinbeck when,
far too early in the
story, the boy Jody
wakes in the barn
to find the door blown
open and the sick
pony gone, and
Jody runs in the dark
over the snowbound
hills to find him fallen
and limp and circled
by vultures, one
perched on his head
already drinking the
dark liquid of the pony's
eye. It's here we learn
that love is innocent,
that death falls
softly sometimes

Boy

like snow in the blind
corners of the heart.
And before I know it,
I've thrown the book
across the room,
abandoning that kid
to the dusky wastes.
And of course I can't
leave him there, and
I also can't keep
reading. Is this what
being alive means,
John Steinbeck?
And what is left
for me to do? but
get up in the dark,
trudging blindly
through the wind
and the tumbling
flakes, and find
that boy.

My Unimaginary Friend

George Oliver

My friends had always been transparently envious of Molly, even if they weren't verbalising this. But it was obvious.

It wasn't like she walked off the page and suddenly interrupted everyone's lives. Molly Bloom's real-world genesis was a slow process, conducted in a far corner of the earth that was only accessible to most of us via the media. No-one was quite sure of how or why she started existing and what to do with the fact. News headlines and word of mouth informed my book club of her existence in the real world long before she appeared on our doorstep, a tattered copy of James Joyce's *Ulysses* under her arm as a tool in her desperate appeal to the only people who might understand her. By bringing the novel that she's a fictional character in, Molly thought these people might *accept* her.

Everyone else she came into contact with for the unknown months and years she was out of the picture either reported her to the police, laughed in her face, or pretended she and the social interaction they just had didn't exist. Or worse: they didn't even realise who she was, which was probably the most common interaction. These people went back to living their lives, while Molly returned to the streets, wandering aimlessly, hopeless, alone.

Once she was *in* the picture, Molly's warmth and generosity was unparalleled. Perhaps this is why I was so drawn to her and why my friends who travelled from all over the country for the book club so swiftly turned on both of us. Try as I might, my friends had never received the same level of attention and interest, despite their attempts to impress me with their book tastes and photos of their room-filling paperback collections, which I always appreciated. Some even claimed that their favourite book, like mine, was *Ulysses*, which was an instant friendship clincher until it became such a repetitive opening gambit amongst new members of the club that I stopped believing those who made such a claim.

I remember the day Molly turned up: it was wet and autumnal despite being in the middle of summer. It was our usual fortnightly Wednesday evening slot of 19.00–20.00 at the town hall, just as that week's session—a discussion of Sheila Heti's *How Should a Person Be?*—was drawing to a close. As was typical of our club, we had frantically skipped to the final page of Heti's book in the final ten minutes of our discussion in the hope that it would provide some form of closure to the conversation.

Molly appeared at the window, drenched and dishevelled, banging against the glass so hard that she nearly gave us all heart attacks. We let her in, put the kettle on, and proceeded to run over our allotted time by eighty minutes while she told us everything. Her story in her own words, ending with a plea for secrecy, for privacy. She wanted a discrete existence that would allow her to be anonymous.

Annie, the town hall's caretaker, cleaned up around us and we never got round to setting next session's reading from the shortlisted books nominated and voted on by the group. We were collectively transfixed by this new story and the fact that the rumours were true and the fake news not fake: Molly Bloom existed beyond the page, alive and breathing. And she had chosen us as her refuge.

After everyone but me grew tired of Molly receiving all the attention and begun to feel very differently about her, she did everything she thought might win over the members of the club, despite her limited knowledge of how to socially interact in the twenty-first century, within the context of a book club and in just about every other one.

Over the weeks, she started nominating titles she loved from her era, written by the authors she admired as much as her own Joyce: Woolf's *Mrs. Dalloway*, Fitzgerald's *The Great Gatsby*, Hemingway's *Farewell to Arms*, Faulkner's *The Sound and the Fury*. Molly's selections were invariably downvoted and soon specifically addressed, despite the club's unwritten rule not to pass judgement on both selected and disregarded book nominations. We were a democracy, as I had been reminding the group since the club's inception nine years ago, no matter how many members came and went in that time.

Sophie (52, Berkshire) addressed the elephant in the room without naming it. It was a warmer Wednesday in September, shortly after I had begun reading out the unsuccessful nominations for that week and before diving into our discussion of the successful one, a continuation of our growing Canadian interest: Rachel Cusk's *Outline*.

"Why do we keep nominating '20s books?"

(Everyone knew who Sophie was talking to, even if she didn't make eye contact with her).

"Yeah, we covered that period *years* ago," Maddie (46, Gloucestershire) offered.

(I waited before diffusing the situation, as was a self-appointed responsibility of my leadership).

"Yeah, and we've *all* read Faulkner," added David (50, Worcestershire).

Molly then tried the inevitable, hesitantly writing *Dubliners* in faint pencil on her small slip of A4 lined paper one Wednesday in October. When this was unsuccessful—which was unsurprising, as the group rarely favoured story collections on account of their range and multivalence—Molly scribbled down *Ulysses*, feeling that she had nothing to lose, thinking that the manoeuvre would be considered a generous opportunity rather than an egotistical self-interest.

"Well...can't say I'm surprised," began Miles (46, London) as I introduced the selections for next week at the end of that week's session.

"Yeah, she's pulling our leg, right?" added Marcus (44, London), going as far as giving the person we all knew he was referring to a pronoun.

"How are we supposed to read seven-hundred pages in a fortnight?" asked Karen (56, Yorkshire), genuinely incredulous, even though when I first met her she claimed to "love" the novel, telling me it was an "all-time fav" ever since she "studied it at university."

I made no secret of the fact that Molly had developed into my best friend over the weeks since that rainy Wednesday in August, so perhaps I had invited the waves of discontent and atmosphere of hostility. I rushed straight over to her after each session, audibly inviting her and no-one else out to drinks, meals at my place, trips to the cinema, more. Sensing that her precarious living arrangement at a youth hostel was about to run its course, I then invited her to move in with me while she figured out what to do.

On a chilly Friday night halfway through October, as we began eating the Thai food that was handed to us on our doorstep, Molly folded her entire hand and threw in the towel: "I can't do this anymore. I can't bear the looks and accusations. I can't take any more exclusion. I...I want to leave the book club."

(I didn't even pretend to lie and say that she'd be missed, or that the club wouldn't be able to go on without her. To be honest, I didn't care. I'd lost interest in the club. I only cared about Molly. We could leave together).

"I've been waiting for you to say that."

Later that week, something strange started happening, and continued to happen for the days and weeks leading up to my generating the courage to step down as leader of the book club and tell the group that I'd no longer be coming...but also beyond that date, for the days and weeks after.

One day, Molly is the one to externalise her feeling of dread, which I admit to sharing as soon as she does so.

"I...I, erm, think I'm being followed. Every time I go to the shop or into town, I see the same black Bentley Mulsanne. The worst part is that the driver saw me see him two days ago, but he was back again yesterday."

(I begin formulating a comparison between this and the surveillance anxiety she and fellow *Ulysses* character Blazes Boylan might've felt while conducting their fictional affair, but scrap the idea while it's still in my head, realising that it would be inappropriate right now).

"I think I'm being followed too."

"Do you think Karen told someone? Or Sophie?"

"I don't know."

We leave two cups of tea to go cold while I try to calm Molly down and help her plan next steps. We're in this *together*, I reassure her.

I win her over, making it clear that she's safe inside these four walls.

"I...I can't go back *there*," she says, even though I insist that we don't know who's following us nor what they want. They could be here to help, I suggest, optimistically.

"I can't go back there."

"Where? What do you mean, Molly?"

"Everything's black. Nothingness. Running down corridor after corridor of nothingness. A broken voice reverberating from all sides around me, stuck on a loop: 'Stately, plump Buck Mulligan came from the stairhead. Stately, plump Buck Mulligan came from the stairhead. Stately, plump Buck Mulligan came from the stairhead. Stately, plump Buck Mulligan came from the stairhead.'"

"I won't let you go back there. I promise."

"Thank you."

Closing Windows

Don Edward Walicek

Our first date in the community garden, the finches
in the rafters that night, their notes floating like confetti,
        turning over,
  over
      and
      some staying upside down,
                landing

       like a   b a l m

         moving into
         different   colors of   skin,
      fading

            in
      the sensation of being together,

        for   good.
How we lay, lips sealed, in awe of those sounds.
How they inflected us, & our mutual understanding
of what *for good* could be
as we found one another, motionless.

Closing Windows

Was it the moonlight dancing across my eyelids
that kept me still, or your kisses in the mirror,
toes to ankle, then inch by inch up into the back of my knee?
You gave me strength, even when you pushed me away.

But now, seven years later, you stand up, shake your head,
& vanish in silence, with so much haste.
Why do our beginnings still hold me without trembling?

Going back again, was it you belting out boleros
in the shower like giant hibiscus
that remade us in full bloom?
A few of those songs echo between these walls, unable to rest.

Afraid they too might leave, I close the windows.
They ask for poems about their history.
But for now, I write stanzas about how I want you
—with me, resetting the clock, & still.

The Worst Time to Discover Something Ugly in Yourself

Devon Borkowski

You're sitting on a dryer
Not running but trembled
Tumbled and shook by the pound of party music
Rhythmic bodies and colored lights
And he is in arms reach for the first time in four months
And you can't stop reaching

The dryer shakes under you
You think of orgasms
You think of sorority house horror stories
Outlining your inner thighs like butcher cuts
Draw black lines around what flesh still moves

The party thrums
The drink line moves
And he ducks under your arms for a picture
You tease and poke and try not to probe
And he said *listen, honey*
All cut teeth
Sharp and snide

The Worst Time to Discover Something Ugly in Yourself

Listen, honey
Listen,
          Honey
It could kill you
He could kill you and he would
With those half lidded eyes
Your heart beat tastes like warm beer and copper
Climbing up and out your throat
     Listen
Honey
          Listen, honey
The twist of his mouth
And the way he smells still lingering in your hair
             Oh god—oh fuck

Crossed wires spark on contact
          Ozone
    And battery acid
You are left alone in the aftermath
Of your own private lightning strike

To Be Made of Hunger

Zackary Medlin

The juvenile eagle wheeled above us, this
one pushed farther inland by want. We
watched it carve the sky in its slow hunt,

gliding as a form of self-preservation,
keeping in reserve the necessary
expenditure of itself needed to feed.

My friend turned to me, said something
I remember as "to be animal is to be made of hunger"
regardless of what his actual words were,

because he was young and walking always
as a poet in the woods. The raptor was starved
to nothing, which I think is the natural state

we're all born into. Because it was a new
season, and I was young in the way I knew
my addiction, I tried to take everything

for metaphor. When the eagle began its dive
away from being my vehicle, it angled
its wings tight around the tenor of its body,

wore them like an echo of itself. As it vanished
in the canopy of the spring's budding birch.
I knew in a moment its wings would billow.

Because this was another season I couldn't leave pain
-pills, I was practiced enough in *shadow*, in *clutch*,
that I didn't need to see to know the eagle will

pull away, so as to only just touch the river.
Still, its talons will cut the water into ribbons
to drag a grayling or whitefish from just below

the surface. That's why we were there, too,
though each of my casts was a craving
more than hunt. A few I kept and gutted,

for most, I eased loose the hook to release the fish,
as if pushing a body away from me was enough
to assuage the useless hurt my hunger caused.

Una rama cae precisa

(original poem, Spanish language, Argentina)

Carolina Esses

Una rama cae precisa
en el espacio que le reserva el aire.
Cae o se deja caer
en un único movimiento.
Una ola, quiebra el silencio como una ola.
El eco de mi repetición, cansa.
Quisiera caer una sola vez y con una sola palabra
pero todo se prolonga más allá de lo ordinario.

A branch falls in the exact

(translated poem, English language)

Allison A. deFreese (translator)

A branch falls in the exact
space the air has saved for it.
With a single motion, it topples
or lets itself drop.
A wave breaks the silence like a wave.
How tiring the echo of me repeated.
I would like to fall just once and with a single word
but everything expands beyond the ordinary.

Sky Woman: Seasons

Melissa Michal

Spring

She stands on the hill, high, high atop the tallest peak. Down below, she sees grass and trees and plentiful flowers. The wind blows through her long, long dark hair and her ribbon skirt which touches the grass, billowing them back and forth together in unison. Her shirt, tucked in, balloons out a bit too. The designs call back to times gone before. She wears what was back then and what connects now in this moment to the people. Her colors, although muted, call to purples and whites and grays, poking out in the deepest green of the grass blades, which also wave in the wind.

The hills roll before her, blanketed with green all let go to nature. Spring's flowers have already popped up with crocuses, violets, and glory-of-the-Snow flowers, all matching her skirt. The tip of the breeze lingers the possibility of crabapple, lilac, and cherry blossoms soon to arrive. Everything floats around her.

A road winds its way through one of the hills and she stares its way, waiting. Trees behind her whisper, gathering their leaves together in chorus responses with the wind. A few birds join in with their throttles. But she focuses in on that road, her eyes following the lines marked on a gray pavement. The only modern indication for miles within her eye range. She can remain there for long periods and often does. Just waiting. Just holding on to the idea that somewhere down there are relatives.

They seek pathways. She remembers the winding days, wondering the right steps forward and how to make connections. Ancestors see what she sees, too, but she likes this spot, alone.

And now she sees all. The hills her guide. And sometimes the hills act as natural walls. For not even she can see absolutely all. But thoughts of those below rise to her mind, rise to her consciousness and she desires to respond. If she stretches her eyes, she can see all the pathways, all the winding roads, and all their varieties of flowers and medicines. She places her feet ever so carefully each step as she watches from this spot. Quiet, soft steps offer her opportunities to listen more clearly.

Nothing yet. Her ears catch the familiar morning dove coo, and she spots the white pine and the maples that will soon flaunt their leaves. Some varieties are forever gone, some have evolved, and some remain steadfast through all the changes. She has learned not to be too surprised at what might appear in her vision next.

Her feet never tire of this land and she does not sit. Sometimes, she changes her regalia. Sometimes, she changes from where she watches. But this spot, this highest peak, is her favorite. She recognizes the most from this perspective. She can name the nettle leaf, the strawberries, the different squirrels and chipmunks, and she even believes there are trees there, hidden from her relatives, that they think gone.

Perhaps not all is lost. Perhaps there is merely someone like her waiting for an opening. For one moment of connection, with a quiet call that runs along the ear canal and connects her to each relative. Each pulse of blood.

Summer

Heat sits along the land and weighs in waves on the air, on the trees, on the tips of the hills. The clouds dissipate, leaving the sky a brilliant blue as if the surfaces should be lighter and brighter. But the heft of the temperature permeates. Her skin no longer feels this pitch of warmth. Some would say there is no skin, no body where she exists. But that isn't entirely true. Souls remember.

She holds her hand to her forehead, squinting through the haze. There are cars coming now, more and more each day, crowding the spaces with their engines and their exhaust. Pushing their sounds away from herself, she walks to the edge of the hill, letting thoughts rise and enter her ears and her being. Taking them all in, the words moving fast sometimes, other times mingled with tears, or anger, and sometimes just pure, full joy, she braces for the sentences to become part of her.

The ribbons are wider and more abundant in this skirt that touches the ground and remains still unless she moves. They move down the skirt in a rainbow, as if she plucked all of the worldly ribbons and sewed them there. Columbine and daisies and buttercups now mix in with the violets. Echinacea and chamomile and lavender flourish below her eye line. Shade hangs over her head from the old, old oak tree. A white pine wafts its sap scent her way, also part of her shade. But the sun still penetrates through the branches and right into her eyes. Haze and sun then mix, and she imagines sweat trickling down her back and arms.

A hawk calls above and floats the drifts, followed by the old eagle crying, a return to the area strengthening below. But the eagle never left where she stands. He wakes her each morning, opening her eyes and ears. A grey tree frog trills somewhere in the far distance. It's mating calls make their way up to her because she can hear beyond her eyes and beyond her place in the sky. The hills are so high, they nearly float there, haze masking them from some human eyes.

Trees are silent today, however. The stillness of the air is her least favorite part of the summers. She misses the calls the branches make back and forth to one another, and the way the leaves dance and sway and sing. This used to be her longed-for season when she stood down with her relatives. A pushing up of stalks and flowers and herbs. An arrival of abundance and sun and warmth that set through to her bones. This season she had felt the most alive and the most useful bringing in food and creating meals for her family. And the dancing. How her feet tapped the earth, tapping down, patting it in circles and more circles.

If she listens carefully enough right now, she hears the faintest of drums and rattles. They will be dancing and preparing food. And there are more drums and then...then there are voices rising up to greet her ears and tickle her eardrum. They seem so full of joy and she wishes to join.

There on the hill, she cannot dance and sing with those relatives below. If she chooses not to watch, not to wait for them to speak to her, she could go dance with other ancestors. And sometimes, she thinks about doing just that.

The singing continues, but something adds to some of the voices, and she hears different tones rise within the singing. Some sorrow. Some anger. Some confusion. Questions. Longing. Moments of pain or shame mingle in with the beats. And this, this is why she waits. A time to listen. A time to process their needs and prepare something to return to them. Something to give them peace and hope and renewal.

So she stands, taking everything in. Listening.

The songs help her remain steady, keeps her feet planted momentarily, even though she is meant to dance. The waves of music wrap around her and hold her. She closes her eyes and settles in to the words, the phrases, the sentences of both the music and the people calling to her. Their emotions enter her, yet she can syphon them out as belonging to certain souls, their spirits so individual in tone.

She breathes. Heat rises and rises and touches her. Her eyelids flicker with different colors. In and out, she breathes again and readies to return her messages back to her relatives across the land.

Hope envelops her, asking them to listen, passing that hope out beyond the heat and haze. And her body steadies.

Fall

The wind blows her back, pushing her, while her skirt becomes its own balloon, almost rising her up and back at once. Fire orange and red waves stitched into the yellow calico produce a quilted fire pit around her feet. She cannot move without crunching leaves, leaves which swish loudly behind her, brushing against one another.

She matches the oak leaves and her button earrings beaded into trees represent her connection to its roots. She has been listening awhile to her relatives. Their cries. Their prayers. Their gratitude. Their desires for change. Their fights for justice. As the wind courses over her, she breathes deeply, holds her belly, then lets it out, then pulls it back again.

Her eyes closed still see the myriad of rainbow colors change as each relative's voice rises to her mind. To her chest. And when the two spaces connect, she opens and finds herself sitting cross legged in each person's mind. Sometimes it's a dark space. Maybe there is a table lamp, or a comfortable chair. Other times, she floats in a field of corn or flowers or a forest darkened only by tallest branches above from old, old growth. Sometimes the person appears briefly or simply stands there. She reaches out her hands, waiting for them to take her offer or to at least touch her palms.

When they do, there is so much light. Her words then enter their thoughts. She will sit there as long as they need her to, while simultaneously being with another relative. Everywhere and in one place with one focus. All her energies put into being one mind. Thinking forward outside of themselves.

She stands on the edge every day to intentionally be outside of herself...even now still thinking forward.

Smoke wafts up from household chimneys and burning wood marks the cooler weather moving in slowly over the land. The air sends misting rain down. She feels the chill, but does not leave her connections. Her relatives both need her and don't need her. She holds space where she passes on her words and she sends them back their own rainbows.

Leaves swirl around her head in the storm's coming. The mist will soon turn to rain, tamping down the grass, the dirt, the fallen leaves, and the dying changes of fall.

Winter

When the winter snows blanket the land, much might be covered, however, she can now see the true outline of the hills, the valleys, the roads, and rooftops. Smoke rises still from certain houses that are lit from within. Light pops up in the windows, yellow and bright white across the snow. The consistency of the white reveals shapes, shadows of people in the windows, and footprints of those having taken early morning trails. Maybe hunting. Maybe caring for animals. Maybe a solitary walk.

The pink and yellow light touching the tips of trees and chimneys softens her own pose, relaxes her body. She pulls the fur-lined coat closer around her body. Deerskin boots cover her legs to her knees. Embroidery lines her leggings in flowers and mountains, white outlining brown.

She turns and heads behind the oak and white pines where there are trails. Some lead further up toward the ancestors. There are her footprints there from some time ago. The other direction leads to her relatives down in the hills. This is the way she walks, her boots making gentle prints that the snow will drift back into and cover within hours.

When she approaches one of the houses after a long, long walk, smoke curls up out of the chimney. Wood stacks up by the door, neat and only piled high enough for the needs. The curtains part from the window overlooking the backyard and woods. Shortly after, the door opens.

A woman stands there her hand on her hip. "It's really cold out today."

She doesn't feel the cold. But this woman can't know that. The woman opens the door and waves her inside. "My mom always said that when a stranger comes by, you give them food. I just pulled some bread out." She keeps her back turned while walking to the other side of the tiny house into the kitchen.

She latches the door and follows. A wood stove glows orange as she stokes the fire in preparation for her guest. The woman stands and then looks her over. "My name's Erin Skye." Erin doesn't hold her hand out. Instead, she cuts two large hunks of bread and pulls butter from the refrigerator. A bit of rust shows on the old model that is otherwise quite clean. The kitchen, too, smells of pine and tobacco. Herbs hang from the ceiling along one wall and sage burns in the corner. Wood-paneled walls keep the home's cabin appearance.

She smells cedar amongst the pine. Erin has placed her best wood in the stove. "I'm Sky," she says.

Erin continues to observe her carefully. She shoves the butter dish over to her along with the knife. She smooths the creamy spread across her bread and hears it crunch, the bread in the center gives way easily to the knife. Just how she remembered. Soft inside, crusty outside. She chews ever so slowly and can taste the salt, cream, and grain and raises her eyebrows. This is unexpected.

"Have you been out there long?" Erin asks.

"Yeah. A while."

"Those boots are very old school. My grandfather made them that way." Erin chews her piece of bread and eats it more quickly. Her eyes never leave her guest.

She finally realizes why this feels familiar. Erin's voice has called to her. Many times. All reasons. There are no pictures of her daughter and son, the center of many prayers. The home has simple furnishings with just a wooden table for four, a small couch and chair, table lamps, a basket of knitting, and one container potentially filled with beads. She can't quite see that far. Erin wears no jewelry. Open shelves line the kitchen stocked with canned goods and a set of dishes and mugs.

"Cozy," she says.

"My great-grandfather built this. It's an old fishing camp in our community." Stacks of papers sit on the counter, all the same size. Flyers. There is an image of her daughter on the top paper.

"Would you like some more?" Erin asks. Her hands are calloused. She doesn't wait for an answer and cuts them both another two chunks. "I prefer it warm. Lately, it doesn't make it to dinner." She chuckles and her eyes light up.

"Do you have neighbors?" she asks.

"Down a bit. Just far enough. I grew up with these families. So we look after one another. You know. Out here, you have to. Our grandparent's trapped here together and then fished in the summers." Erin finishes her bread quickly again.

She takes her time as the kitchen stove's heat impacts her to her own surprise. The neighbors Erin mention, she has also heard often. Pockets of community are easy to spot.

"You like the bread?"

She nods and makes a groaning noise.

The woman laughs. "Yeah, it's popular."

"The right crust to soft bread," she replies after savoring the bread in her mouth longer than usual. "Your family must enjoy this, too."

Erin closes her eyes a moment. "Most have gone. My son lives with his wife on the other side of the country. A few cousins the next city over. That's blood, though. Lots of people are family."

She nods and admires this woman. Her movements between joy, anger, sorrow, and passion are the reasons she stands on that edge so long. All of them are. She takes Erin's hand and squeezes. Erin's eyes widen. "Thank you," she says. Erin's energy passes through to her once more, but this time, her skin offers a new sensation.

"Just bread," Erin replies.

"You so easily open your door."

"Just the right thing to do. What else is there?" she says.

She puts her coat back on. "I should go," she says.

"Here." Erin wraps the rest of the loaf in a cloth. "It can warm your hands." Her hand holds her guest's hand for a moment.

She leaves the house. Erin is right, her hands remain warm. She heads back into the woods and then leans on a tree. For years, she watches Erin hang flyers, hope and anger mingling in each staple to a board or post. From the hills, she knows their experiences, but cannot feel each one in her body at that distance. Not like this. Her chest is hard, like a ball bouncing around.

Her footprints along the path filled with snow. And she knows what brought her down here. Her heart has been seeking the connection. The clouds formed by her breath start to dissipate. The climb is long and her feet crunch, patting down the snow. When she comes to the top, she realizes the time has been quiet up and back. She pauses at the point where she either goes to watch over the world or where she can visit the ancestors. Her relatives have others like her and she heads to the ancestors for a time. That night, she dances with Erin's daughter and hugs her, passing on her mother's energy. Then she gives her the bread. Her daughter smiles, holds the bread in her hands, and stares down at the package. Then her daughter touches Sky Woman's cheek and she can feel warmth, just like her mother's.

Later, she returns down to her spot, her skirt in full winter white and her spirit still warmed by the stove and her stomach full of bread.

We Are Here Together

Benjamin Green

I can hear the snow piling,
And while I wish I could
Run with wolves and leave no trace,
I know, come morning,
I will trudge to the wood pile,
And back, carrying loads
Of soon-to-be-heat,
Leaving a muddy path in the knee-deep snow,

But, now, the trail I am on keeps winding,
Deepening into the pallor of day.
A swirl of darkness, of snow,
Closes around my body.
Ice ridges on the sides of my boots.
I trudge on, noisily.

There are birds in this air,
Slowly turning in the cold wind,
With wild eyes and furious
Incensed cries of anguish.
For a moment, I think I have left the earth,

But I am here: I know,
Because the birds sense me;
And my skin, my hair, their feathers
Rise, prickle, tremble.

On a trail suddenly black,
With snowflakes the only source of light—
The birds let me know
We are here together.

Barcelona

Peter Serchuk

There is a beautiful place in the mind that rebels;
that one day wakes incensed by the prison of straight lines,
the politics of right angles. Suddenly, everything inside
seems a pantomime of passions while outside, familiar trees
mirror a garden of old ideas. Before you've said a word,
you're suddenly out on your own limb, casting a shadow
unrecognizable even to yourself.

If this happens to be your mind, now may be a perfect time
to visit Barcelona. Built by Romans before Christ descended,
it's been crowded from the beginning and restless ever since.
With your new shadow, you could walk streets that have reinvented
themselves time and again, learn to shout *no més* in perfect Catalan
and fall under the spell of Cases' *Julia* or Fortuny's *Bastián*.
In Barcelona, rage and love sleep in each other's arms.

Then again, the climate is not for everyone. The summer heat
dizzies the eyes and the Mediterranean does little to cool the blood.
Miro's *Pla de l'Os* may put a soul at ease for an afternoon,
but once you're out on a limb, Barcelona is no place for rest.

Barcelona

If the beautiful place in your mind has spoken, if it vows to never turn back, perhaps it's time to remind yourself, as Gaudí often did; there's triumph in a certain madness and a vision remains in every masterpiece, even those left unfinished.

Abrís los médanos con el revés de la mano

(original poem, Spanish language, Argentina)

Carolina Esses

Abrís los médanos con el revés de la mano
para ver por dónde sigue el camino. Yo voy detrás.
La casa permanece erguida en su borde de líquenes y rocas.

Un peregrino caminaría con más cuidado.
Un náufrago sabría que la arena no es tierra firme.
Somos los únicos que se mueven de espaldas al mar.

Entre la espuma crecen racimos de algas
fosforescencias...regreso sola a la orilla.
Y esta bien, pienso, si la luz
de nuestra ventana se apaga y uno de los dos
al menos, está ahí para juntar los restos.

Ahora tu cuerpo es un punto entre las dunas
ritmo constante de aparición y desaparición.
No deberías darle la espalda al mar.
La playa es el mismo océano que nos expulsa
hecho arena.

You part the sand dunes with the back of your hand

(translated poem, English language)

Allison A. deFreese (translator)

You part the sand dunes with the back of your hand
to see where the path continues. I follow you.
The house stands at the edge of its rocks and lichen.

A pilgrim would tread more carefully.
A castaway would know sand is not solid ground.
It's only us who continue with our backs to the ocean.

Through the foam, clumps of phosphorescent seaweed
grow...I return to the shore alone.
And it's fine, I think, if the light
from our window flickers out while one of us
at least, is there to collect the remains.

Your body is a dot between two dunes now
the continuous rhythm of appearing and disappearing.
You should never turn away from the sea.
This beach made of sand is the same ocean
that ejects us.

Fighter

E. Laura Golberg

I find the ATM is broken,
request the bank staff post
a sign, which they refuse.
So the stream of people
in search of cash struggles
for a while, then gives up.
On a deposit slip, I write
"OUT OF ORDER," balance it
on the ATM's keyboard,
later persuading myself
not to go back to check
if it's still there.

Then, there's that fight
with my gym over dirty
mats I thought I'd won
until my disinfectant cloth
wiped off black.

The Triscuit box, its picture
of farmers who grew grain,
only men—I wrote to Nabisco,

Fighter

not allowing myself to accuse
them of some kind of male
immaculate conception.

I'm brittle, my every muscle
tense at the smallest slight.

One Wish

Greg Kosmicki

Quiet evening, few cars drive by in our busy street. Windows open
to let in air, still sweet and fresh, what I know of sweet and fresh.

Somewhere on this planet far away from my fellows,
air would be sweeter, fresher. Still, I am happy

for what I have of it tonight. Like everyone else in this country,
I don't know exactly what's missing, we lose a little fresh air

here, a species of insect there, a plant eradicated by a zealous
          homeowner bathing his yard
in Roundup over here, lines of DNA never repeated.
                                        As soon as I write

there are few cars tonight, they pick up in frequency, as if the guy
          pulling the strings
on all this overheard my thoughts and set things back to rights again,
          ratcheted up the noise

and emissions. Just now a car bass so loud my windows rattle.
          Smoky odor,
someone having a fire pit, drinking beer and telling stories, I hope—

or a burning house. My hope is for the pit.
A simple thing to hope for.

Suddenly, no cars. So quiet it reminds me of something.
I can't remember exactly what it is.

Hiroshige, *Naruto Whirlpools, Awa Province* (1855)

Ricardo Pau-Llosa

Only the effect of depth can be eyed and not
depth itself. That's the evidence of the swirl
in the urgent straits: hollow imprinting the lot
of presence but not its essence. What will
leave fingerprints? It signs only the arrival
of mystery. And so with water, at once fated
to earth but dragged by wind and moon, a rebel
element imprisoned in the rules of hated
emptiness. The sculptural wave will fail
in mid-soar and drunken vanish into a lace
halo. Swells cetacean flatten in a flail
of arms, for all is Icarus in this place.
From rocks we loom to see forbidden turmoil,
free to awe, brave in land's embrace.

Reciprocal Debt

Marco Etheridge

Ted Gretzky—never Theodore, unless you're with the IRS—stands on the metro platform, keeping the maximum distance possible between himself and his fellow commuters. Human beings top the long list of things Ted Gretzky does not enjoy. His list has grown over forty years, but Ted's fellow citizens still hold the number one spot.

Gretzky is a big man, a full head taller than the suit-and-briefcase drones who mill about the platform. Not much of a puzzle how he got that way. Ted's tata, Piotr, was the biggest Polack in the old neighborhood. Cecilia, his mama, was a tall black woman. Her height was only one of many anomalies, not the least of which was being married to a giant white man in a time when heads still turned as the couple walked down any street.

Because Ted looms above them, people don't crowd too close. Perhaps they sense his dislike of humans. Maybe they just need some distance to maintain a perspective view. One can't see Mount Rushmore standing on Washington's nose.

Whatever the reason, Ted waits on his train in a small bubble of space enjoyed by no one else. This special status, along with his extraordinary height, gives Ted a wide view of the crowded platform. That is why he sees what is about to happen before anyone else.

Ted hears the rumble and screech of the approaching train as it hurtles through the darkness. The grimy mouth of the tunnel belches a billow of stale air down the platform, rustling the skirts and papers of the commuters. A stab of light chases the foul air, and the nose of the train appears in the darkness behind.

A scrawny guy darts out of the waiting herd. He's walking fast, a few steps ahead of the charging train. Time freezes. Ted Gretzky sees the train driver silhouetted behind his glass panel. He sees the yellow caution stripe at the edge of the platform. And he sees how this young guy just stepping past him is going to intersect with all of it and mess up Ted's commute.

Ted swings out one meaty hand and catches the dude mid-chest. The skinny punk sort of folds up around Ted's forearm and the big man pivots to bring his left hand into play. He plants his left paw over his right and shoves. The dude backpedals away, arms windmilling the stagnant air.

It's a tiled column that stops him. Dude hits it like a sack of spuds, slides down it the same way that stupid coyote used to slide down a rock wall in those Road Runner cartoons Ted used to love.

The train lurches to a stop and the doors hiss open. The herd of commuters takes one look at the man slumped in a heap, one look at Ted, and then city-dweller instinct kicks in. They ignore everything as if it never happened and rush for the impossible chance of a seat on the metro.

Ted looks down at the mess he's made of this skinny idiot, then glances over his shoulder. Down at the other end of the platform, he sees two transit cops showing an interest in what's happening. The cops are heading his way, weaving through the crowd of drones that pulse out of and into the train.

The big man curses under his breath and bends to grab the fallen would-be jumper. Ted doesn't like human beings, and he likes cops even less. It's not that he's doing crime on the streets. Piotr and Cecilia raised him too hard and strict for any of that nonsense. Naw, Ted follows all the rules all the time, not because he likes rules, but because he doesn't like to talk to cops. Ever. About anything.

He yanks the little dude to his feet, gets one arm wrapped hard under the guy's armpit, glad to feel the guy's heart beating in his birdcage chest. He frog-marches the asshole toward the nearest exit, hoping the punk isn't seriously broken, that this guy maybe took a shower sometime in the last week, and that the cops are too lazy to follow. He half drags, half carries the dazed would-be jumper up the stairs.

Emerging from the Metro station, Gretzky gets lucky on all three counts. The cops are nowhere in sight. He drops the skinny guy on the nearest bench. The dude is breathing and he's staring up at Gretzky with big stupid rabbit eyes. And he looks reasonably clean for a hipster. Hard to tell since these white dudes like to dress like homeless guys, but least he don't stink.

Ted waves a thick finger in the guy's face. The dude blinks his eyes like he's trying to figure out why someone stuck a kielbasa in his face.

"You stay, hear me?"

The white guy frowns at the big finger under his nose, then looks up at Ted, manages a nod that seems coherent.

The big man walks away, muttering under his breath. Stupid white guy messing up my schedule. Not like I don't have better things to do. And now I'm buying this asshole coffee. Guy's probably one of those trust fund babies. Million dollars in the bank and they wear clothes look like they sleep under a bridge.

The old Greek is at the window of the Athena. Like where else would he be? Ted orders two coffees, carries the blue-and-white cups back to the bench. The dude is still there. Ted lowers himself to the bench and the thing creaks under the added load. He holds out one of the coffees.

"Hope you like it black. If not, cream and sugar are over there."

The scarecrow takes the coffee, doesn't say a word, not even a thank you. Ted sips the coffee, waits for what he thinks is an appropriate space of time, and gets nothing. The asshole is just sitting there holding his coffee, staring at a pigeon that's mooching around his feet. Ted does not have time for any of this shit.

"Yo, strange white guy, do you talk or what?"

Guy blinks at the paper cup he's holding in his hand like he's never seen such a thing in his life. Takes a couple of big swigs from it, his Adam's apple bobbing up and down. Then he looks up at Ted like he's never seen him before.

"Strange white guy, that's the best you can do?"

"You got a name you like more, feel free to give it up."

"We're like buddies now, or what?"

Ted shakes his head just like Cecilia did when he tried some sass on her.

"Not even close to buddies. I just stopped you jumping in front of a subway train. While we're at it, I saved you having to explain that shit to the cops. Oh, and I bought you a damn coffee. So, yeah, I think we're on solid ground for an introduction."

He looks away from Ted, stares into his coffee like maybe the answer is floating in there. Nods his head, looks back up.

"I'm Tyler, Tyler Ruskin."

"Ted."

Then there's one of those awkward pauses. Ted wonders what the hell he's let himself in for and why he's doing it. The stranger beside him salutes Ted with the half-empty paper cup.

"Thanks for the coffee, and for the other thing, too."

"You wanna tell me what that was about? I mean, what happens if I get up and leave? Do you run back down there and wait for the next train?"

"So, Ted, you normally ask so many questions?"

Ted hears the smartass tone in this guy Tyler's voice. Smartass would usually piss him off in a huge way, but instead, it makes him chuckle.

"Normally, I don't talk to people at all if I can help it. But here we find ourselves, new buddies and all. And one of us just tried to jump in front of a train. So yeah, I got questions."

"Okay, fair enough. I got a problem."

Ted's eyebrows and Tyler's hand go up at the same time.

"Wait, just listen. I get it, someone tries to off themselves, obviously there's a problem. But I'm not some broken-hearted putz throwing himself in front of a train. To quote the head docs, I suffer from Impulsive Control Disorder. They call it ICD for short."

Ted has an automatic bullshit response, a gift handed down by his tata. Ted remembers Piotr's rough complaints. All these new syndromes, Theodore, Bah! This is just excuse for bad parents with lazy kids. These are made-up things, fairytales.

But Ted isn't Piotr. Sure, he dislikes adults, but he enjoys working with kids. Does some volunteer coaching, helps out on a couple of city youth programs, that sort of thing. He knows kids who struggle with one of these alphabet syndromes, good kids who puzzle over written directions or have to work extra hard on homework assignments.

Right, so give this Tyler the benefit of the doubt, at least for the moment.

"Sorry, to hear that, Tyler. Nothing with an acronym is good news. ICD, IBS, IED, they all suck."

"Right? No one wants to hear that. It's weird that you mentioned IED because that's a good way to describe my fucked-up brain. Like there's an improvised explosive device hidden in my head. I never know when it's going to explode, shoot off crazy messages. Hey Tyler, let's step in front of this bus. Tyler, what do you think it would feel like to sail off this balcony?"

"That really how it happens? Shit just comes out of the blue like that?"

"That's how it works for me. My doc tells me some people experience it differently. They're walking past a jewelry shop. Next thing they know, there's a five-thousand-dollar charge on their visa card for a watch they don't even like."

Ted's listening now, nodding his head. He finishes the last of his coffee, tosses the cup into a trash can beside the bench.

"Tyler, I'm not trying to be an asshole here, but you're seeing a head doc for this shit, and yet here we are. You know what I'm saying?"

Tyler spreads his arms, mea culpa.

"Yeah, I know how it looks. And I was making progress, too. Hard to, but it's true. You gotta understand, Ted. I don't want to off myself. Didn't and don't. That's not how this sneaky shit works. It's more like this overpowering desire that pops out of nowhere and then my body responds."

Ted shakes his head again, but this time with something like commiseration. This Tyler cat is hurting, and he doesn't seem like a bad guy.

"You saying you're okay now? I'm asking because I gotta be somewhere. Same time, I'm worried about you. Maybe we should stay in touch. I don't want to lose no sleep over you."

Tyler laughs at this, laughs right out loud. The pigeons at his feet started and flutter off. He reaches for his wallet, pulls out a card, hands it to Ted.

"You're not as hard-ass as you like to put on. You know that, right?"

Ted rolls his eyes, takes the card. Tyler Ruskin, graphics design. He tucks the card in a pocket, stands up, sticks out a huge hand. Tyler splashes the last of his cold coffee at a passing pigeon, crumples the cup as he rises from the bench. His hand disappears into Ted's and the two men shake on some unspoken deal.

"Okay, Tyler Ruskin, later for you. Gotta tell you, weird way to meet someone. No repeats, hear?"

Tyler rolls his shoulders and tries to crack his neck.

"I don't think I could stand a repeat. I'm going to be aching tomorrow."

"Tomorrow is a good word. Let's leave it at that."

Ted turns away without another word. He walks to the metro entrance, pauses at the top of the stairs. He looks back in time to see Tyler Ruskin walking away.

It's the next evening, one of those perfect evenings in spring that the city offers up maybe three or four times in a whole season. Ted is walking across the bridge, commuting home on foot. It's something he does three days a week. He knows what happens to big men who don't keep after it.

He's out on the long span of the bridge, high above the swirling waters of the filthy river. The lighted skyline of the city rises behind him and on the far shore before him, but the river is a dark gulf between the two.

Ted reaches the midspan of the bridge, the highest point above the water. He has no fear of heights, never has, but in a flash, a wave of vertigo crashes over him. He reaches for the steel railing, grabs at it with both hands. He steadies himself, looking a hundred and thirty feet down. At that moment, it looks like thousands.

Coming out of nowhere, a voice cuts through the spinning sensation in his head. You could jump. It's his own voice, but saying crazy shit, saying it loud, shouting it.

Jump, man. Just to see what happens, feel that sensation of flying. Two steps back, a quick lunge, nothing to it. That little railing ain't gonna stop a big dude like you. Go for it, Theodore. What are you waiting for? Do it!

Ted grips the steel railing as hard as he can, his muscles straining to hang on. Then, as quick as it came, the urgings are gone.

He's panting, his heart pounding in his chest. He blinks his eyes, looks up and down the length of the bridge, tries to figure out where he is and why.

He sees other walkers heading out of the city. No one stops to ask him if he's okay. They slide past him and keep walking, earbuds insulating them from anyone else's troubles.

Ted forces himself from the railing, falls into step with the others. Gotta walk before someone gets the bright idea to call the hotline on one of those phones that line the bridge. He's weak as a kitten, but he keeps moving, keeps putting one big foot in front of the other.

He gets home somehow, doesn't remember much of the walk. Then he's in the hallway of his apartment, shucking off his shoes. He stands at the kitchen counter, pours a stiff drink. The whiskey burns his throat. Empties his pockets onto the counter, sees the pasteboard card with raised letters: Tyler Ruskin. That skinny son of a bitch. What kind of sick joke is this? What did you do to me?

Then the memory of the bridge slams into him, the dark water swirling far below his feet, calling to him. And his memory drags in more. There are unwelcome ghosts in the room now, ghosts uninvited and kept at bay for years. Ted drinks off the rest of the whiskey. He waves the empty glass at them, but they don't go away.

Piotr and Cecilia, tall and beautiful, salt and pepper, sad and watchful. Ted can only say their given names. Has done every day since the funeral. Can't call them Tata and Mama out loud. He can barely think it in his head without doubling over.

Two decades they've been gone, lost in the dark water. The same water which flows beneath the bridge he walks across. The bridge you can see from the harbor, and the harbor that opens into the sea.

They named their little boat *Nimfa Wodna*, the Water Nymph. Piotr loved to catch the silver-bright fish, and Cecilia loved Piotr. That's what they were doing when they died, somewhere outside the harbor on an evening tide.

The next morning, a tugboat found the *Nimfa Wodna* capsized and drifting. Divers searched the waters and volunteers combed the beaches, but the bodies of his tata and mama were never found. Now both of them are here in his apartment, a place they never saw in life.

Twenty years Ted has built and tended walls to keep the world out, to hold the hurt at a distance he can manage. He made a mistake today. Let this Tyler Ruskin guy get inside, and see what happens? Ghosts are passing through walls as if stone has turned to tissue.

Ted tries another whiskey to chase the past away, but the past ignores him and settles in for a long evening. A third drink on an empty stomach tucks everyone in together. Ted's head sags to the arm of the couch and the room goes dark.

It's three a.m. when he comes to with an aching neck and a pounding head. The room is dark and empty except for his groaning when he sits up.

Ted drags himself off the couch and into the kitchen. He chugs a glass of water and waits to see if it will stay down. Then four aspirin chased with another glass of water. Braces himself against the sink while his guts lurch and gurgle. That's what you get. Act stupid and pay the price.

Shakes his head, regrets it instantly, walks down to the bedroom with one hand sliding along the wall. The bed groans under his weight as if it's dreading the coming day as much as he is.

The next morning is bad. Somehow, Ted toughs it out, slogging through his work without making a fool of himself. It's touch and go, but he survives until his lunch break. After he chokes down a sandwich and yet another coffee, Ted fishes Tyler Ruskin's business card from his wallet and makes the phone call.

Ted is expecting voice mail. He's surprised when the phone picks up. Says it's Ted Gretzky from yesterday, hears the hesitation on the other end. Tyler tries to laugh it off. Hasn't been twenty-four hours and you're checking up on me already? Ted ignores the joke, tells Tyler they need to talk, he needs to talk, the sooner the better.

Tyler hesitates again like he's trying to figure out how far this goes. But then he's saying sure, he owes Ted a beer at the very least, suggests a place and a time. Ted knows the joint, says he'll be there. They hang up.

Ted stands on the street with his phone in his hand, not seeing the people moving past him. He shakes it off, pockets his phone, and heads back to work.

It's a mercy when his workday ends. The worst of his hangover has passed, leaving him empty and tired. He heads off to meet Tyler, threading his way through the currents of pedestrians hurrying along the sidewalks. A hard lump of dread is lodged in the pit of his stomach.

When Ted rounds the last corner, he sees Tyler Ruskin sitting at an outside table, a beer in front of him. Ted turns his bulk sideways to squeeze into the narrow space. Tyler is up and sticking out his hand. The two men shake hands and sit.

Tyler is smiling until he gets a good look at Ted's face. Then the smile vanishes.

"Damn, Ted, you don't look so good."

"Don't feel so good."

A waitress squeezes up beside their table. Ted orders mineral water, a big bottle please. The woman nods and disappears.

"So, I'm guessing a rough night?"

Ted nods his head, puts his big hands on the edge of the small table.

"More than rough. And then I made it a whole lot worse. Stupid."

Tyler sips his beer, doesn't say anything. Ted waves his hand like he's trying to brush something away.

"Yeah, so thanks for agreeing to meet. How are you doing?"

"Pretty good, considering. That probably sounds weird, but it's true. I guess it's like a pressure valve or something. Me doing what I did, you saving my ass, then afterward all that pressure got released. I don't know how else to describe it."

Tyler takes a long draw on his beer, his eyes on Ted. The waitress returns with the mineral water, pours it, steps to another table. Ted drinks off half the bubbly water without a pause, then refills his glass. The silence grows longer.

Then words are tumbling out of Ted's mouth, out of his guts, and they keep on tumbling. He tells Tyler about walking the bridge, the dark water below, the voice in his head, terrible compulsion to jump.

He doesn't stop there. He talks about losing his parents, the grief of not having their bodies to lay to rest. About the walls he built to hold his grief at bay, and the ghosts that haunt him despite his walls.

Ted blurts all this out to a total stranger, a guy he's known less than a day. He wants to stop himself, but he can't. And with the words come anger and then blame. The blame looks for a place to settle and finds the man sitting across from him.

"What I want to know is, what the hell did you do to me?"

He expects anger in return, something he can push back against, something to refute his confession to this broken guy who is just sitting there listening to him. That's not what he gets.

"I'm sorry, Ted, sorry about your parents, sorry about your grief. That's a heavy load to carry around. But there's something you've got to understand. I don't have the kind of power you're talking about. I can't curse people and I sure as hell can't fix them. If I could, I'd be fixing myself. I've got way too much of my own grief to bother throwing curses on other people. And for sure not on people who just saved my life."

Ted's anger deflates like air from a balloon. He's left empty and wrung out.

"I'm telling you, I don't know what to do with all of this. It's not working anymore."

Tyler holds up his empty glass, catches the waitress' eye, looks back at Ted.

"I think we're going to be here for a bit."

"Yeah, so it seems. Look, sorry I dumped on you like that. Not a fair thing to do."

Tyler waves it away.

"Don't worry about it. I've done my fair share of blaming other people for my troubles. Besides, I owe you. Mean, I owe you a life, right? The least I can do is listen to your troubles."

Ted laughs, and it startles him as much as it startles Tyler.

"You think that's funny?"

"No, not funny. Something else, maybe. A life debt is what they call it. Like you owe me a life, or I owe you a life. I forget how it's supposed to work."

Now it's Tyler's turn to laugh and he does.

"That's not a real thing, you know. People talk about it being ancient wisdom, but life debt is a Hollywood thing, like Han Solo and Chewbacca."

"That doesn't work cause you're not big enough to be a Wookie."

Then they're both laughing, and something evaporates in the laughter and drifts away from their table.

"Okay, Tyler, I get it. The life debt thing is bullshit."

He hesitates but says the next thing.

"That doesn't mean we can't be friends, right?"

"Nope, nothing in the rules preventing that. So, from one new friend to another, you need to know that I'm one messed-up monkey. I've had other yesterdays."

"I get that."

"What I'm not is any kind of mental healthcare guru. I'm a recipient, not a provider. So, friend to friend, you need to be talking to someone about this load you're lugging around. You owe it to yourself."

"Same goes for you. You owe it to yourself not to jump in front of any more trains."

Tyler nods his head, then holds a hand across the table.

"Then here's to reciprocal debt."

Ted reaches for his new friend's hand.

Your Downstairs Neighbors Are Having a Party

Violet Piper

the distinct anthropoid melody of introductions
ascensions, descensions, exclamations, yesses and nos
oh, yes
ah, no

the mating rituals transmit over the bass and high hat
defuse upward from the molding, into your dresser, between the folds
      of your sweaters.
that swell and swallowing, decided by the position of the door
aaH
Aah

the noise explodes out from your past
simulates every adrenalized approach and panicked abandon
impersonates every party you missed or weren't invited to
every silhouette of your crush on the other side of the room
every Instagram story recorded from the pit at Barclays Center, angled
      up at the stage and
weaving in between the other phones like a stalk in a cornfield

Your Downstairs Neighbors Are Having a Party

Goodnight.
downstairs,
they escape together

and upstairs you escape alone.

Shrinking World

Myles Weber

A boy with perfect posture sits
where faculty and students
get laptops debugged.
His computer works fine.
He is waiting on a companion
to walk to the cafeteria
or back to their dorm rooms together.
I take a number, sit down, and
imagine a life
with this boy as my son.
I'd challenge him
to excel at math, of course.
The books I'd press on my child
would be the dangerous ones
upon which the next book builds
and expands his frame of reference
so widely it ruins him
for girls his age.
Religion I would approach
as both an artifact
common to every surviving culture
and a portal to the mysterious and true

so my son would retain
the generosity of spirit
that compels him to sit here
and wait for his pal in silence.
Most men my age marry,
sire children in the flesh.
One of my generation raised this boy,
who stands when his buddy reappears.
As they head out
I envy their agreement
to waste a part of each day together.
That afternoon,
I meet an acquaintance on main street,
ask if he will wait
while I step into the drugstore
to buy a paper.

Sorry—I haven't time.

He runs off, comfortable alone
in all matters but his home life.
I've got him beat.

Trying to Close the Blinds

Judith H. Montgomery

I thought I could tidy that room of my life
as though it were the last lodging

of the missing or the dead—strip spent flowers
from a vase, set each insistent picture

straight on an invisible shelf. Shut the blinds
to keep the sun from changing dark

to light—but even as I linger in the hall, latch
clicked behind me, your body breathes

inside mine, as once, on Lake George's shore,
and zipped against wind in our sun-flickering tent,

we lay, skin to skin, within—then stilled, quiet
after rapture, despite the fervent birds

overhead, the water's sip and surge, the distant murmur
of others brewing coffee in the old tin pot...

Trying to Close the Blinds

I can't close the blinds. I'm no more exempt
than any body left behind—the news

of your passing passes through, and through me,
like a half-shuttered lantern's flash

across plashing waters. Here are you. Still. Stilled.
Gone. (Not gone.)

The Moose

Zackary Medlin

A dead moose lies partially
submerged in the Chitina
River's slate-blue water.
Bottleflies frenzy inside
& around its empty sockets
until the corpse appears
to stare from mosaic eyes
not unlike a fly's, glistening
stained-glass iridescence.
Their myriad carapaces
are almost a holy beauty.
Also, an apocalypse.
They lift from the skull
like a black veil, beneath
the fevered buzz, the flies'
music is both hymn & dirge.
The song sung in water
carries away questions of how
or why. This was just a life
swept up in the rush it tried
to wade. The current doesn't ask
whether the body is dead

The Moose

from want or accident,
doesn't count the pills
in the stomach's contents.
Nor does the current care
that, a mile or so downstream,
we are lifting the water
like psalms to our lips,
swallowing the decay,
not yet knowing the death
coursing through us.

I Am Trying to Like My Life Again

Devon Borkowski

I am trying to like my life again
I take the children out for dinner
And I don't yell when they lay down under the table
And get lint in their hair
And kiss me with their ketchup-chocolate milk mouths
The little boy leans on my shoulder
He tries to pay the cashier with a connect four chip
He holds a sticky hand to my cheek
Like I used to do to my mother
It smells like french fries and I take his picture
His little ginger head warm under my chin

I am trying to like my life again
I learn how to buy my own plane ticket
I go to England and drain my bank account
And watch the sunrise come up through Stonehenge
I flirt with a taken man and it doesn't amount to anything
I send nine post cards
And buy one extra that I don't fill out
I get sick in an airport bathroom
I don't tell anyone but my mother
Who texts me to take a Tylenol only after I've boarded

I Am Trying to Like My Life Again

I watch the stars past a stranger's shoulder
Through the little porthole slip of sky
They are closer than they've ever been

I am trying to like my life again
I go for breakfast with my brother
And I tell him too much
I say too many honest things
He laughs because I have always been careless
He asks me *why, just...why* and he doesn't want me to answer
I am crass and terrible and delightful for him
And he worries for me but doesn't say
He pays for the meal with our father's card
We agree not to buy each other gifts this year
We walk together to the car in the rain

Advice

E. Laura Golberg

I am cleaning my boots
and the leather is cracked.
I ask my husband's advice.
He takes the boots from me,
"Thank God" they sigh,
and the Boot Connoisseur
finishes the task.

I remember Berthe Morisot
who asked for advice
on a figure in her painting
from her brother-in-law,
Èdouard Manet. He took
over the brush and finished
the figure himself.

More than the Parts

Michelle Hartman

Rain constant, heavy occasionally
nudged sideways by small gusts of wind
falls on a park bench, centered between
two light poles, their yellow-tinted glow
valiantly fighting the dark,
way above their cheap, city-provided paygrade.

Wood slats in three curves, with metal legs
managed to appear lonely, sad. Top curve
lends a pouty lip to the picture.

Most only see rest spot
mugging opportunity
rack for the homeless.

Yet, there is a fascination
to these pieces of serviceable furniture.

More than the Parts

They are probably the Universe's largest
repositories of raw potential.
People meet here,
        first times, thirtieth,
                proposals, breakups, to remember.

On sunny afternoons agents swap secrets,
documents, eating their tuna on rye.
Spinsters read their romance
novels over brown bags, chai tea
they wish was a gimlet on a Paris balcony,
prays someone, anyone will sit next to them.

Hope has soaked the wood, maybe
the surrounding ground and spindly sapling,
swaying in gentle wind nearby light
post and bench.

Possible like faith,
hope is a kind of madness.
Not dangerous,
simply the source you need
to stand up
and walk forward again.

The Cat that Crossed the Wetlands

Scott Beard

It's another night in the rainy season when the bands of low pressure roll east and deliver their slow, steady faucet drip across Okinawa prefecture. The wind blows and Akemi is awakened from the same dream in which Lolly, the six-year-old Lynx-Point Siamese that her father had given to her for her sixth birthday, is bludgeoned to death by the falling arm of a rotting oak when the curious feline scrambled over to the ancient tree to hide from a predator chasing after her.

Akemi lies on her back, double checks between her legs; the moisture is only sweat. She wipes her forehead, pushing the writhing strands of dark brown hair from her eyes. The rain hitting the roof impersonates boxcars on steel rails. She listens to her heart race. She fidgets in bed, trying to release the tightness in her arms and legs. Her chest continues to pound. She puts two fingers on the inside of her wrist, slides them back and forth to wipe the perspiration that has settled there like dew on summer morning grass. She turns and reaches for the water on the nightstand. The clock reads 5:24, and she brings the glass to her lips with shaking hands; the water undulates around the brim. She sips, but the tunnel vision has started, and she sets the glass down.

Breathe. *Yasumi*. Rest.

She steadies herself, inhales slow, heavy, and listens to the rain batter the roof. Her head hits the pillow again, but she cannot go back to sleep; the image of the terrified and broken feline from her recent somnolent state steadily lowers the melatonin levels in her brain, and it's only a short while until the black of night eases into a dripping, gray dawn. She reaches for her cell phone and checks the weather; the storm will push through by mid-morning.

Her mother enters in her business suit. She carries her briefcase and green umbrella in one hand and a pile of Akemi's clothes in the other. Akemi sits up in bed. The patter of feet whispers from the closet and Lolly rambles into the room, her little grumble erupts from the wooden floor and ends with a plop onto the pile of clothes on Akemi's bed. Her tail undulates and she rubs along Akemi's leg. Akemi scratches the cat under her purple collar and Lolly purrs. Her mom watches, her small smile on rounded, olive cheeks. Her mother tosses the pile of clothes at the end of her bed. Lolly darts under the covers. "Ohayo."

Akemi runs her hand through her brown hair. Now, her mother is staring out the opposite window that overlooks the hills and the dark shadows that cover the miles of birch, elm, willow, and maple. The rain and clouds engulf the tallest trees. Her mother turns. She is looking at a family portrait of herself, Akemi, and Akemi's father. Lolly meows from the tails of the comforter under the bed and peers out. Her mother turns. She watches the cat for a moment, sighs, and walks to the door.

"Ichinichiju nenaide." *Don't sleep all day.*

Akemi smiles. "Watashi wa shimasen. Sayonara."

It's quiet again in the house. Lolly peeks out and hurdles the clothes and onto the bed. Akemi strokes the cat which has curled up on her chest now. The rain still plays its monotone on the roof, and Akemi sits up to look out the large windows by the stairway.

Beyond the rooftops to the south, Akemi sees the large oak with its gnarled arms stretching from a bent trunk, a sentinel to the rolling grass and brush that canvas the open wetlands that stretch east toward Peace Memorial Park. She used to climb it once a week until she was eleven or twelve. That was something she had learned from her father when she was young. She was about four when she first visited the park with her parents for an afternoon picnic. Her father and a group of the elders from the Ryukyuan people performed the *Zo-odri*. They walked and danced to the rhythmical strums of the sanshin, its sturdy strings fashioned from the algae reeds harvested from the Sea of Okinawa.

Akemi was fussy that day because of the blazing sun and humidity that had blown in from the eastern Pacific and she tugged on her mother's arm and wailed, imploring through gritted teeth and salty tears to leave. They walked along on the blazing gravel underfoot, her father holding her hand, stopping at spots shaded by the spiraling spruce trees, and her father would lift her onto a low, dangling branch, arms extended as Akemi ambled it, waiting to catch her, lowering her to the ground. He smiled at her, holding her in his strong arms, laughing, "You are always so busy girl." He lifts his arms upward, takes in a deep breath, lowers his arms and exhales. "This exercise will help you be at peace. Now, yasumi!" *Rest.*

Now, Akemi yawns, stretches her arms over her head, and tosses the phone between the soft pillows. Lolly grumbles and jumps to the floor. Akemi showers, gets dressed in her blue jeans and a t-shirt, and makes the slow descent into the main floor—the living room and kitchen and indoor porch complete a square—one large room. The room is encompassed with windows on all sides. They overlook the village and out across to the wetlands. Breaking clouds still hang over all of Okinawa, puffy and black on the horizon to the west. In the kitchen, Akemi pours water into a cast iron pot, places it on the gas stove. She waits. Her mother has left the windows open in the large living room. Akemi glances at the wet rooftops that dance along the undulating foreground around Mabuni Hill. To the east the sun tries to peak over the tall trees, and the vapor trails form little rainbows that blow in the wind across the hills until they disappear against the black clouds lingering on the horizon behind her. A white egret flies into her view, its delicate and awkward wings flapping like book pages in the light wind. She watches it sail toward the oak on the horizon where the sky clears to a rich blue. The remaining gray cumulus drift on the light breeze until they blend into the horizon over the wetlands, its foreboding trees swallowing the clouds into a gray blanket. The water hisses on the burner when it breaches the pot. Akemi shudders and looks down. Her hands tremble. She sighs and walks to the stove, reaching for a burlap bag from a cabinet above her and unfastens the drawstring. She smiles, tilting the bag toward the boiling water. She watches a few grains of rice trickle from the burlap bag into the water. She fills the pot halfway, reaches for the kettle on the stove, fills it with water, and flips the back burner on high. She turns to the window, lifts both arms, making a circle with every inhale. When she completes the circle by meeting her fingertips at the top, she exhales and retraces the circle with her arms back down to her sides.

The kettle steams and Akemi returns to the stove. She flips the kettle burner off and smiles when she sees the rice steaming. She lifts the pot, taking her time emptying the water into the sink. She sets it back on the cooling burner, retrieving two eggs from the ice box, cracks them over the steaming pan of rice and tosses them in. The yoke curdles in the pot. She takes a slotted spoon from the drawer and stirs the eggs and rice, reaches in the cupboard for a large bowl, and pours the eggs and rice into it. This was her father's way of preparing eggs and rice. She opens a drawer and retrieves a pair of chopsticks and sits at the lonely table that serves both the kitchen and dining area.

Lolly scuttles in and prances at her feet before she can take a bite. Akemi smiles. "Kiti, kiti."

Lolly's tail sways. Akemi clamps a clump of rice and eggs with her chopsticks and feels the cat brush across her leg one way, and then retrace her steps. She reaches her free hand underneath the table and runs her hand across Lolly's back as she passes. Lolly purrs. Her father always loved to listen to the cat's mild vibrations.

Akemi eats in silence. She inhales the wet maple from the rain when the breeze wafts in. It brushes her back and the tickle forms goosebumps on her arms. Even in the heat of the summer the sweat is cool. The goosebumps are like little embers forming from her father's simmered hog over a bamboo fire, the smoke and heat rising from the center. She remembers his hunts in the wetlands for the best male boar, using the traditional Okinawan method of yamashishi-yai, her mother diligently dicing the goya melon for her champuru, seasoned with sea salt—crushed and extracted from rocks along the Sea of Okinawa.

Suddenly, Lolly breaks Akemi's *shuchu* by brushing along her leg. She meows and circles. Akemi sighs.

"Okay, okay, hang on."

Lolly grumbles again and follows her back into the kitchen; meows intensifying when Akemi reaches for a can of tuna and fills her dish. The cat purrs and carefully picks chunks of her breakfast out. Akemi strokes her back for a moment, then grabs the dishes and goes to the sink.

She takes her time, using a washcloth made from banana peel fibers called basho fu that her mother had stitched together, lathering it with bar soap sold at the Northern Okinawa market. Her father never liked the foreign soaps you could get at stores, they always dried his hands out and made them itchy.

Carefully, she dries them and places them in the cupboard. She heads back into the main room, sits down in the old chair by the fireplace. Her father's yari hangs above the mantle; he last used it four years ago, the last time he had gone on an *inoshishi karu*. Akemi shudders and turns back toward the kitchen.

They found him late that night. The moon shone through the deep blue spruce and on writhing limbs and the undulating hills of the wetlands where the snorts and grunts of the phantasmagoric black boar dwelled. Her uncle, Katsuki Tamei, had arrived at their house. He usually waited on the porch for Akemi's parents to welcome him in, but he entered noisily. The cries broke through the living room and Akemi's mother was out of bed in her morning robe. Her mother closed Akemi's door, and she was left there with Lolly. Akemi trembled at the wails from outside on the gravel drive. She didn't leave her bed that night. Lolly stayed by her side and purred when Akemi ran her fingers through her yellow and gray fur. The soft strands smooth on Akemi's hand, and her eyes became heavy as she stroked the cat. Finally, she closed them, hoping that she would see her father in the morning, cradling a bloodied hog in his heavy arms, but she never saw him again.

Now, the doorbell rings and Akemi leaves the yari in the living room. She runs her hand through the locks of her long, brown hair, sighs, and heads to the door. It's only the postman. His blue plaid uniform shines its familiar pattern through the panes. Akemi smiles and slides the storm door stop latch to hold the door open. A strong breeze picks up and the packing slip on the top of the box flaps and sails away in the wind. Akemi brings the box in and sets it on the kitchen table.

She returns to the open door. The postman has retrieved the slip. He walks back to the porch and hands it to Akemi.

"Arigato." She smiles.

The slip is addressed to her mother. From the manufacturer's designed box, there are images of women with their hair pulled up in traditional dance style. Akemi grabs a knife from the drawer and slits across the taped edge and pulls the adhesive across the folds of the box. She carefully removes the Styrofoam from the box and sets it on the table. The ceramic pot has been fired twice with a clear glaze for prolonged use. Its white background subtly blends with a light gray and gives the illusion of a dull purple when not in direct light. Several dancers are dressed in a white skirts and red blouses, puffed along the shoulders and at the hem of the skirt to allow the performer to move unimpeded throughout the kabuki. The ornamentation wraps around the pot asymmetrically, and in the background, small Bonsai trees rest in four places on the pot. Akemi knows they represent the change of the seasons, life to death and death to life; and the dancers, in the forefront of the seasonal sentinels, mean that life will always go on, no matter what. She smiles when she looks at the photo of her mother and father resting on the shelf, the same trip to Peace Memorial Park she had remembered that morning, just a few days before she had gotten Lolly. She laughs. "Kiti-kiti."

Silence.

Akemi walks to the kitchen. "Kiti-kiti."

"Lolly?" She clicks her tongue on the roof of her mouth.

Akemi walks to her bedroom, ascends slowly. Cumulus clouds slide their way in front of the sun and the hallway grows dark. "Kiti, kiti, kiti, kiti..."

Only the breeze in the tall palm branches outside responds.

Akemi reaches the bedroom. Her bed lay as she had left it, covers half off, the pile of comforter at the foot of the bed on the floor. The blanket is pressed down where Lolly had lain that morning. She bends down, feels it cool on her hand. She walks to the closet. "Lolly." "Lolly…kiti…kiti…kiti…"

Akemi's face flushes. Her stomach churns. She rambles down the stairs. The storm door is open, swaying in the heavy breeze. She scans the living room. "Lolly!"

She heads to the door and slips her tennis shoes on. She is down the porch steps; the faint clouds wafting slowly west toward Peace Memorial Park. She walks the perimeter of the house; the grass is wet and the dew sneaks through the tips of her shoes. The grass blades cling to the rubber sides, washing away the newness of them. "Lolly!"

The panic attack comes. Her hands tremble. The blood pulses in her veins. Her chest heaves. Akemi closes her eyes, thinks of the smiles from her mother this morning. She is fine. Her chest slows. She pictures her hand running through Lolly's soft gray and yellow fur, her large whiskers, the calm purr, and Lolly rubbing her face along the side of Akemi's hand. Her breath returns.

On the ground, a small, purple collar lies in the high grass leading to the forest. Akemi picks it up, squeezing it in her hand. Tears form. Slow, steady, like the kind she cried the night her father left with his tribal spear on his final hunt. Her chest heaves. But in a moment, she is not consumed. Her teeth grit, she waits. She has not been in the wetlands since her father died; its dark overhang and writhing limbs like haunted shadows from that night four years ago. She wipes her sweaty palms on the sides of her jeans. She remembers her cellphone is where she left it in bed. Akemi exhales, loosens her jaw. Her feet rest softly on the muddy earth oozing through the thick grass.

The wetland forest is dark under the canopy. Further along, a creek forms along an embankment. Akemi dances through the high grass and reaches the moist soil lining the side. The water runs swift from the storm earlier and it rushes along, splashing on the bank. The mud cakes the bank and Akemi inspects it. Several small broken prints canvas the mud. Her pace quickens. She lifts heavy legs over fallen limbs, weaves her way through tall, wet grass. The forest thickens and even the fog from the morning rain hangs on in the canopy. Up ahead, an outcropping of trees canvas the forest. She stops in the high grass. In the center stands an old, spindly oak with its branches writhing arms. She knows this tree. It is the same tree from her dream this morning. She remembers the tired arm of the old oak cascading down.

"Lolly? Loll...eee! Here kiti kiti kiti!"

Silence. She waits, staring at the tall oak ahead; its arms stretch out like tentacles. Then she hears it. The snorts break the silence. Her hands tremble. Her chest tightens. The brush sways and whips from side to side. The rustle of leaves and snap of small limbs closes in. A pointed hump of grizzled, black fur crests the brush, and its head appears, its tusks like giant spears. The hog snorts, bucking its head. Akemi's chest pounds. But, through the fog, a weak cry breaks from the mass of oaks behind her. She sees Lolly's undulating tale and alert eyes, her soft meows churn. Akemi's heart races.

Lolly is hunkered down on the rotting arm of the oak and a whine escapes her. Akemi cries. "Lolly! Oh my god, Lolly!"

She rushes to the tree. The hog starts out from the brush. Its hooves kick up mud; it paces back and forth, the saliva slithers from its slimy tongue when it growls. Akemi trembles and she steadies herself on the large trunk of the oak. Lolly has climbed to the large, lower limb now. It is too far for her to jump. Further out from the trunk, the outer branches hang low. Akemi jumps, pulling on the lowest branch. The bough bends in the middle and Lolly grips the trunk, claws deep into the rotting oak. Akemi gets a better grip and she's able to pull herself up, arms and leg dangling from the breaking branch. It cracks under the weight. The hog snorts and charges for them. The bough breaks and they fall. Akemi hits the hard earth below. The limb lands in front of her, its twisted arms shield her from the hog. Akemi screams. The hog bucks his head and jams at the downed bough. Akemi presses her legs up against the downed bough, keeping it in front of her. The hog snaps and snarls through bared teeth. It rams the bough with its head and the branch begins to split. The hog is pressing into the breaking limb when Lolly jumps down onto the back of the wild boar. She hisses, clawing and swiping at its coarse fur. She manages to scrape its nose and her claws gauge thick flesh. The hog snarls and whips its head back and forth. Blood flies through the sultry, forest haze. It bucks and steps back. Lolly screams, darting back to Akemi's side under the twisted and broken bough. Akemi cradles her in her arms. The hog snorts. It cannot reach them under the bough. It paces the tree. Lolly growls. Akemi yells, clenching her fist into the wet earth below her, flinging mud and rocks into the face of the panting and growling hog, its eyes fiery red, like the eyes of the hogs that her father had hunted, watching, waiting, in the thick fog of the deep forest, striking fear into another generation of hunters, of brave men and women of Okinawa, forcing them back to the safety of a warm bed, tired, broken, and alone. Through the mist and darkness, Akemi can see her father there with her strong, brave, his light smile channeling away the fear that races in his heart, and he thrusts his sharpened yari and the hog. Akemi grits her teeth and reaches for another rock. She hurls it at the hog, hitting it across the bridge of its nose. She throws another and another, landing sharp blows across the hog's body. Finally, it turns and bolts away back under the canopy, disappearing like a memory into the fog and dark of the wetlands.

Akemi lies on her back; her heart pounds. Lolly grumbles and crawls onto her chest, nuzzles her face. Her tail waves and she purrs as the fog slowly fades.

In a moment, Akemi is on her feet. She scoops up Lolly and carries her in her arms. She knows the way out. She has walked this forest many times with her father. She hears his voice along the winding stream that will lead them back to their home. Lolly purrs and Akemi listens to the slow whisper of the stream. Soon, they are back on the edge of the Bermuda grass.

The front door stands open. Her mother, home for lunch, waits at the head of the slow walk up the gravel path. She holds her hand to her face. She kicks off her business heels and makes the descent from the porch steps. She runs across the damp Bermuda. Akemi fights tears. Lolly meows and her tail undulates as her mother holds out her arms.

"She...she got out. I had to...I had to go look for her. She was in the forest. There was a...there was a hog."

Akemi's mother covers her mouth with her hand.

Akemi speaks between sobs. "I couldn't just leave her. I couldn't just let her go."

Her mother pulls her close. She cradles Akemi's head to her chest. The tears stream down Akemi's face.

Lolly squeezes out of her embrace and hops to the ground. She purrs and rubs along Akemi's leg.

"You've had a long morning my child," her mother says. "Do not be afraid. Now, yasumi." *Rest.*

Her Week in Paris

Bethany Reid

"God knows I never sought anything in you except yourself.
I wanted simply you, nothing of yours."
                    —The Letters of Abélard and Héloïse

Only that spring Notre Dame had burned,
the great spires crashing down. But always,
she knew, the entire world was slipping
toward entropy, everywhere a patina
of ash. Protestors in yellow vests,
soldiers in bruised blue and black,
their weapons dragging down their hands.
She rode the Métro. She bought
ice cream on the Left Bank, pretended
a few hours was enough for the Louvre.
Winged Victory one morning and another
the medieval tapestries at the Cluny.
It was a kind of insanity, trying to take
all of it in. Afternoons, she walked up the steps
in Montmartre and in the shadow of Sacré Coeur
she sat at a sidewalk table and ordered in her poor French
un café, sat with her notebook open
and didn't write. She wanted to say something

about Père Lechaise, another sort of museum,
art of the chiseled stones
or of the bodies lying in quiet rows
beneath the earth, each its own ruined cathedral,
the graves of Jim Morrison and Oscar Wilde
littered with tributes. It was raining
the morning she visited the cemetery. Héloïse
and Abélard did not lie there
according to her guide, only their effigies
carved in stone, almost hidden behind thistles.
She'd wanted to crawl through the fence and spend
an hour pulling weeds. She could dedicate
herself to this city, even in ruins, like a nun
to a lapsed God, or like the cleaning woman
she'd seen at the Musée d'Orsay,
dragging along her bucket and mop,
handmaid to a daily astonishment.

The Maid's View

—Joan of Arc at Coe's Circle

Suzy Harris

This time of year, I stand in darkness
at four in the afternoon and watch
the city close up around me. Bikers
in their black shrouds surround me,
round and round the circle they spin

then fling themselves home,
leaving me standing here alone
through the dark night. Do I rest
my gilded eyes or keep watch?
Do I imagine my younger days

enthroned on a real gold-clad horse
leading the charge, trampling
the innocent underfoot? I tell you,
it was not my intent, but it never is,
with war, to trample the innocent.

The Maid's View

I do my penance here on this bronze steed,
where rain cannot quench my thirst,
food does not satisfy my hunger. Just when
I think I can stand it no longer,

the sun rises above the housetops
torching the clouds tangerine and honey,
lighting another day, and I am still here,
standing tall, to see it.

Disoriented in Portland
—after Kim Addonizio's "Here"

Vivienne Popperl

After the heat dome ended *it got so much better*
which took a while of course but still
the days grew shorter and we're so grateful
which *tells you something about how* the weather
has changed so much in Portland that sometimes
we don't even recognize where we are anymore
it's as if we're now in Northern California
my husband says, which has some advantages
because the warm days stretch on into the fall
and we bask sleeveless in the sun in November
but then the trees seem to be taken aback, many
still holding on to their leaves, glowing yellow
orange, red, long after leaf day has come and gone
and the streets, swept to bare black, glisten in the rain

Earthquake Woman
—after a Chehalis story

Madronna Holden

One day blind old Earthquake Woman
was rocking her daughter's baby
in her arms while her daughter
was away on the prairie
digging roots.

Trickster's girls came along
and saw that baby and wanted it
for themselves.

So they snatched it, thinking to fool
that old woman by setting
a rotten log in her arms.

But Grandmother Earthquake
cried the tears of lava
the earth hears as prayers—

she had fire enough in her
to melt stone—

her song was strong enough
to wrinkle up time.

So she instructed her daughter to carry her
while she sang her power.

And when she lifted her mother up
that young woman found herself glowing
as if seeded with stars.

She found herself
stepping over mountains
to go after her stolen child.

Pebble

David Capps

The pebble shows its smoothness on every side, turning in our hands, its grain, silica, flecks of quartz, is the grain of the sun as it first appears on the horizon. It is the ocean's wearing down, tile to a sandpiper's burrow, sand dollar disguise to a starfish as it elongates from one shadowed rock to the next. What it becomes when you take it in your hand, when you caress it: a part of a whole, a living stanza of a mythical suite, source of wave and ripple as it skips, or drops down into the heart's half-paved abyss, it is an echo given shape, made solid, granted a reality that makes it no longer 'it'.

This was a project we would do together, we would complete, though my grandfather did most of the work, careful not to let my small hands get too close to the machinery. The memory is foggy, but we must have used a lathe, a drill, and some machine for punching holes into the cardboard backing of the knife display case that began as unfinished pine boards and ended with the varnished finished project, down to the lock and key. My grandfather Artis had the heavy yet graceful hands of a machinist while mine have developed (atrophied?) into the hands of a writer and musician. They fidget when they aren't writing or stroking a beard, or exercising pressed against the strings. They fidget the way a mind filled with uncertainty fidgets, grasping for a pebble to hold onto.

The thing about the pebble, any pebble—and I don't mean a chattering pile of pebbles, a pebble beach such as you see in postcards

Pebble

of places no one visits—is its uncanny eloquence, its ability to know when to stay silent and when to speak. You could even just stay: its ability to know. A forest cairn you see assembled together details the wizened expressions of pebbles. One says the wind descends from the mountains, another that it follows the river, the third that it skips across the western plains, so that together they stand, in silence from all sides. All equally confident, oblivious to changing winds. The smallest cairn has six eyes: one for each cardinal direction, one up and one down, and one inner eye which makes the cairn indestructible; or nearly so.

Though would you want to be indestructible, meaning not subject to sense, to judgment, validation? Why should stones not write in all possible languages of touch? When an Aurochs' eye from the Ishtar Gate collapsed in the arms of the grass, the outermost lash of the ruins, those by the ledge—glacial hooligans, stone peepers, little wonderers fallen apart, heads buried in flint axes, they all came out to see it. Is this what devotion does, or love, a gradual smoothing down, so that the contours of the mosaic can no longer be seen or touched?

At other times the pebble's expression is quite inscrutable; like it doesn't want to say any *particular* thing, yet doesn't hold anything back either. Perhaps it's tired? Indifferent? Or perhaps having reached that level of equanimity we can only hope to catch a glimpse, it no longer feels the need to speak. Then the need to speak means one lacks self-sufficiency. When I was a child, I thought my grandfather capable of everything. It was his factory. He had built it. We spent a few hours each day for a week or so (it seemed longer) on the red factory floor, the drone of presses around us, safety goggles on, until it was finished. He was clearly proud of our (his) work but there was no need to be self-congratulatory. Once, before my grandmother was senile, and before my grandfather was completely debilitated (he was gradually losing motor function), I remember my grandmother asking him if he just wanted to go for a drive, how he acceded although for him there was no afterlife, nothing beyond, there was just the thought to please her for ole times' sake. But it was the same when he was well, that responsiveness. When we had wanted a merry-go-round for the backyard he had been there before you knew it, pouring the concrete foundation. The tall frame of a swing set still stands beside the tree outside my dilapidated childhood home.

I find myself then speaking in my own way of his equanimity, that he never swore, never was upset, never said a harsh word to anyone. Although it must have been a thing to suffer in his condition, to face the irony of losing the ability to speak just as your grandchildren were reaching the age at which they become interesting to speak to. Unmoved by the outside world, the greatest joy can resemble the greatest sorrow, to be withdrawn into oneself unchanged, or to have made contact with that which is non-self, leaving behind that same body which might ask in the grip of sorrow: what does this body matter? This same question can be rephrased so that it is half-smiling: what does this body matter when I am unchanging? In the small stone statue of the Buddha on my desk I see the stone's sly smile. After he had lost his motor function my grandfather would sit in his easy chair watching and not watching Baywatch with the same enigmatic smile. Maybe that is why I keep little knickknacks, as reminders. If I chose to toss them all more would accumulate. And if not, then ideas would. For what is a stone smile to the inner glow of the Buddha, or even the idea of the Buddha?

My grandfather's knife collection he had tucked away in a drawer on the nightstand by his bed. There being unseen lent them majesty, power, the aversion of the gaze idealized, submission to the authority of Artis, or art. Then we would sit together and carefully unpack them from their cases, the antique Bucks, the Case knives, Swiss Army knives, giant bowie knives, West German makes from Solingen, PA Steel Co., those with bone or antler handles, pearl inlays, switchblades and butterfly knives, fishing knives equipped with ice picks, and my favorite: a terrifying curling shiv he had made with a bright blue molded plastic handle and sheath made of masking tape.

It's hard to imagine beginning with something so functional and then attempting, through successive generations, to ornament and ornament the thing so that only the slightest trace of that original functionality remains, so that it is hardly noticeable anymore, or gives way to ideas, archetypes: hardness (did I really know what a 'Rockwell factor' was?), solidity, sharpness, fierceness, edge, the beauty of shining in darkness. It's a pattern you see begin with flint knapping techniques, where the stone is gradually refined, made symmetrical, deadly, made to impress some particular individual who belongs to our collective prehistory. The pebble I'm taking about, the one that has the moon reflected in it (not the Man in the moon or the rabbit moon, just: moon), that lies at the bottom of a crystal clear lake and is seen by no one: that is its perfection.

At that time I had a rock tumbler I believed could bring out the best in each unpolished stone, though there were many bumblers, pockmarked irregulars, which I asked to join me in the summer along the shore. Reflections glimmered like moonlight walking across pitted stones of itself, boring into the cool water of its shelf when I reached my pink hand in and eons went tumbling by, behind those pale blue veins of a child's wrist, dozens of stones I carried back, including Petoskeys, their paeans chalky, muffled hymnals smoothed by the grain; by grain or the grit or bolt or silt, my boyhood parishioners singing on without guilt. I suppose it is, or can be, the same when you are with someone: you can feel like yourself, you can feel confident, even if you are the object of someone else's pretend, even if afterwards the voice no longer sings and the mouth hangs open, a memory of someone else's step along the way.

Fossilized coral, hexagonaria percarinata found in the Alpena Limestone rock strata, accounts for the bursting star-like appearance of Petoskey stones; before continental drift, when my home state of Michigan basked in the warmth of the equator, long before Pleistocene glaciers plucked them from the bedrock, there among the sheltered clams, cephalopods, crinoids, trilobites of the Devonian reef, the fragile arms of this coral burst through the sea's living brine, knowing the compass that is sunlight. Seeing it and being seen. Only the mouths are left, hexagonal faces silenced by time, by time turned to calcite.

In one of the only photos of my grandfather I remember, he is holding my older brother in his arms, his hair lightly tousled in the wind, side by side on the wooden swing, the one with aluminum soda cans crafted into airplanes with wind-spun propellers hanging from the frame, gently rocking into a kind of futurity that I think must be instinctively understood by a new parent, or a new grandparent, that says: there are precious few times like these that come in life, and in savoring them you knew it, as trite as it seems, 'they grow up so fast' or 'ho hum' or 'everything's good'.

On windless days I remember grandfather's A-frame cedar shed: the heat of the heart's faint pulsation, the sun's restless occupation shriveling grapes into raisins; the endless curiosities: cherries, crab apples desiccated on the window sill, still boulders inched along by your finger's impulse the power of motion; they were firebrand dreams changing from red to black, living to dead, sawdust gobs hanging from spider webs, never developing beyond themselves, never changed into anything like you saw in the distance, spooked Goldie galloping with her thick mane and white tail as the dark clouds gathered, grandfather watching over me even as I watched over him.

The name 'Petoskey' derives from the Ottawa word 'Petose-gay' meaning: 'rising sun' or 'rays of dawn', or 'sunbeams of prom-ise', which Chief Neatooshing had named his son after seeing how the sun's rays fell on his son's face. There were stones that could have been part of my depths, had I had the strength to skip them across the clear waters of Lake Michigan, the dull strength to take the largest, lob it forward, in; to walk beside you in a way committed, the way my grandfather walked arm in arm with my grandmother, his brown eyes as deep as a swallow's, gently humming along the same shore as all of us, towards the same eternal end, finding some meaning therein.

Our own basket full of stones the color of moon dust I eventual-ly encased in indoor light. Striations of fireworks, ancient marine lives plotted the lag between explosion and sight. Grey skeletons walked before us, crisscrossed clumps of wormwood, this day spoiled to mock through our teeth the cruelty of defining love. Small waves defining love as cruelty. Sun overhead, a prism spitting spent cherubs, rosy paint from a Titian subject in which love is youth eternal, sand dunes, gestures of bleeding day, flaying the damp June grass.

As you walk along the beach there is a custom of finding and giving pebbles. A stone will claim you, because it knows its size and shape is suited exactly to the one you will give it to, blindly. Then the one you gifted it knows about you, something about your tem-perament, your way that is completely you. The way my grandfather held my hands in his and told me to look carefully as we cornered the burred edge of the cabinet. How on our last day I gave away the Peto-skey stone to the only one I'd ever loved.

Meditation on a Tree

George Rose

It begins with something
as simple as a tree. Take that one
in the middle distance. It's not alone
and in fact is surrounded
by other, more beautiful
trees, and the hedge obscures
the lower half, so it looks as if
it's at some great distance instead of
along the edge of the parking lot.

Across the street from where
I'm sitting, in the patio of an
abandoned cafe, once busy with
conversation and crying babies,
the tree is like a tree, no more.

Nobody notices the tree but me
and I only notice because I happen
to be looking straight at it. I assume
it's not looking back (trees don't do that)

Meditation on a Tree

But if I look at it long enough
and let the tree do the work
then I am in a meadow in Montana
or a green valley somewhere
where far off voices echo strangely, a place
I've been but can't quite remember

And then rapidly, like shuffling cards
associations—with other trees, other
tree-like beings and places begin to
carom off and sprinkle the wider angles
of sight and then a dog barks and
I'm alone in the cafe again and the tree
is just a tree.

Journal Entry: Off the Earth

David B. Prather

Sassafras comes up from the roots of my neighbor's tree,
                                    the lawn riddled
with these sucker plants. My neighbor is a ghost now.

                                    Whoever it is lives
there today, I don't know them. But this tree I know.

                                    My great grandmother
told me she steeped the root bark for tea, reminiscent
                                    of root beer, told me

it was good for whatever ailed the body, whatever troubled
                                    the soul. She also

let dandelions burst across the yard, so she could gather
                                    the greens for salad.
I've never had her taste for what is wild, a bee to its clover,

                                    butterfly weed
to its bright spot in the sun. There must be fifty or more

shoots all spreading
in the shade of these dove-shaped leaves. If I let them,
they would spread

quick as fire. And the trumpet vine on the fence would
grab the corner

of the house, overwhelm the walls, the roof, the windows
and doors. How easily
I could be trapped, a folk story of a man surrounded by vines,

a desperate voice
drifting out of the tangles to lure people in, who are never

seen again. I get
down on my knees in the brittle August grasses, a supplicant
to summer heat,

and I break the sapling stems with my bare hands.I whisper
my regrets

to the earth that only wants to offer new growth. Anyone
watching might
think I'm praying. But I'm not.My great grandmother

may be listening,
her back bent with years of collecting low-growing

curatives. Even
the poisonous milkweed feeds a caterpillar, its body
filling with flight.

Transistor

Laura Ruby

—for AM McLemore

When I was young, I had one of those clock-radios with the alarm
you could set for buzzer or music. I chose it myself, but was surprised

every time I woke up. At my therapist's, I would rail against men
who made a monster of me, accused me of mixed signals because

I refused to be tuned one way, for them, for always—dancing girl,
armless maiden, handless, headless. I told this therapist I'd make

a good man, but what I'd meant was, *I've got volume*, what
I'd meant was, *It's okay to play softly*. People used to call women

handsome, now they only say that when you're too old to save.
Once, someone pretty/handsome told me that all of life is transition.

Water flows in and out, time waltzes its lines across the face,
yada, yada. (I write poetry because I like my failure built-in.)

A woman who loathes other women hisses that the cancer
hasn't forgotten me, as if I could forget the cancer. The Ship

of Theseus sails by, replacing itself. But with what? That's me,
my cells eager to try something new: *We will grow a nose here,*

we will grow a bone there, see what else we can make of this
leaky boat. I have a conversation with a trans man. We chat

about chemical menopause, the kind we've both endured.
Different reasons, same outcome: hot flashes like immolation.

According to the body police, I'm more man now than I ever was,
fists of surgeons' scars and hard-won wisdom. (Handsome.) As if

a man is nothing but a hammer and a woman a purse, people
reduced to the things that swing. The woman at the post-office

double-checks my ID, drums her fingers, croons low, dials in.
"This you? It doesn't look like you at all." Hands over

my package anyway. Conductor, receiver, resistor, I was
wearing a mask, and I was stripped down to the wires.

Ode to 234684

Matthew James Friday

Only a 5G satellite can see you, 234684,
aged just five months, tagged for your first flight
belittling the line between Alaska and Australia,
the adults all gone six weeks earlier. The flock
of first-timers fluttering hearts, tails trembling,
the wait for the favoring wind. How they know
what fronts are forming, the pulsing lay lines
of the hidden remains hidden, a magician's trick.
11 days, 1 hour. 13,560 KM. Praise be to numbers.
No stops, not for bemusement or applause
or delaying winds, storms, the fist of the abyss.
A marathon no Iron Man can manage.
Limosa lapponica. Bar-tailed Godwit. A bridge
between the functional and the divine. Organs
of your existence shrunken to myth so the fat
of the landlocked—insects, mollusks, worms—
can keep you watered. You bulge twice
your weight with lungs so sharp they cut air
only Sherpa knows. Scientist don't know
why you didn't die after 3 or 4 days. Peaked
pectoral muscles, missile shaped. You beat
4BBRW, the twice record holder older male.

Ode to 234684

No tourist you, passing Hawaii by, wings struck
with Vulcan's eye. Unihemispheric sleep—
you're halved and twice the wonder. Did anyone
see you bullet by Kiribati, Vanuatu, track east
of Sydney? What glitter, gut instinct or commune
mind attracted you suddenly right to find
Tasmania. Already mapped out is your March
return: China and the tidal flats of the yellow sea.

Milky Way

Dennis Lum

The reunion for the one who brought us here—
without asking—is the first in years. We hike uphill
and enter, arrange ourselves around her,
held safe at the center of her railed bed.

We hear she hears, so we tell her
about petals on flowers. Her eyes close and we lean back
in our plastic chairs, seek starry night. But the glass
reflects only fenced-off grievances, lava-bright.

We writhe, and then—one long commanding groan
snaps us up, and bits of rusted wire fall to the floor,
that sole chained breath drawing us into her orbit
with its silent gravity. She who spun us into this world.

Do you remember how we fought for the best stick?
Stuck our marshmallows on its tip, held close
to the crackling embers? They warmed inside,
then exploded into the Southern Ring Nebula.

Milky Way

Our newest telescope sees billions of years
into the past. My mind's eye is weaker,
but still my lips rub the crusty edges and my mouth
savors the charred sweet caramel, swallowed too fast.

I was young with you once, when all of us played
and sprayed fire and forgave.

Midwinter

Andrew Robin

'Do you remember foxgloves?'
she says, as if summer were
another lifetime.

We lie naked,
she has twined herself
into a braid

of cold sunlight
crossing uncaught
through abandoned webs.

'How when we were kids,'
she says,
'we would pluck the blooms

and touch
their nectars
to our tongues,

and our hearts
for an hour would go
heavy and slow.'

I say,
'I remember
a fox who

followed me home
from the bus stop almost
every day

and sat with me
in an orchard
while I slept.

I could tell that fox anything.

One day I said,
I don't love you anymore
to see how that felt

and never saw him again.'
She says,
'You ruin things.

You ruined
my story.'

Midwinter

I say,
'I never gave him
a name.

He was too
beautiful,
too

lonely
to name.'

A Mask of Marriage

Bethany Reid

In the early years, the mask
was mornings in bed, two bodies
under one cover, light falling as if through silk.
I was married, *happily ever after.*
My face was the mask I wore,
or so I swore, not raising questions
to needle my better half.
The mask kept me from talking too much,
hooked over and itched at my ears,
reminded me to listen.
A mask of marriage
seemed a useful thing, made much of
by family, by our children,
daughters who grew to want their own masks,
thinking it would lift them, like wings.
Marriage was forever—hadn't my mother
taught me that? And I had all the evidence
of weddings, white dress
like an angel's gown, *till death do we...*

A Mask of Marriage

It feels too late to tear it off.
My mouth is curved downward,
my teeth, sharp. Someone has painted a smile
on the mask. I think it was me.

Not Love

Casey Killingsworth

Scream what you call justice
until it runs down
your leg, feel the need
to care with your fists,
be emboldened by the
quiver of your voice
that keeps shouting
you're right, you're right,
say, "but he's not talking
to me," pick up rocks
to defend picking up rocks,
pledge to a flag made of words,
speak for anybody
else, inhale compassion, exhale
exhaust, I don't care,

but that's not love.

Protocol

Ahimsa Timoteo Bodhrán

Years before Mother
sees him as spouse,
the punk, hoodlum, no-good
that was my father
fails to arm wrestle, bench-press
more than her.
                A member of her own gang,
          he is one war chief she doesn't respect.

Years after he is chased
out of the neighborhood
into the military,
                         he emerges,
                 finally a man, grown up,
                    worthy of her time.

Already engaged,
she lets him talk.
                A year after they marry,
          he, drunken, raises a fist to her.
            It does not land, but he does.

Protocol

Him, within seconds, on the floor,
a knife to his throat.

Mother tells the man
he will never raise a hand again,
or he will die, and
they will never find
the body.

More than any ring,
oath uttered outside the communion rail,
this promise of him obeying
she will keep.

A promissory note.
A protocol for prosperous mating.

Ghost Overture

Nate Maxson

When we think about haunted houses
It's always Victorian, three story mansions, the outskirts of industrial
cities
But here, here
I will give you something
More close to home
What about all the houses
We built and left
In the nowheres of America

Rooms where you can see the blizzard
A face yawning in a descent of far white clouds
Open, wounded, emptied houses
Monoliths rotting on the prairies
Their lightning rods extended like ring fingers
The rotten wicker chairs where we take our seats
Where we watch
The nocturnal animals
Gathering fuel

The Old Haunt

Shawn Schenck

The sky hung a pinkish-orange glow, dense with vapid insect agility. The boys were out. Their shoes pounded against the ground in a constant groove beneath the rhythmic chirping of summertime grasshoppers.

Each of the boys had grown over the summer, filling out their bodies in slightly different ways. Jaden grew 2 inches and sized out of his favorite Chuck Taylors—forcing him to embrace his brother's old British Knights—while attempting to fit into his favorite MC Hammer shirt. Sam, hiding her bodily changes, decided to stop stuffing her hair into her hat and cut it off while happily relying on the thrift store to adopt a more *neutral* look. Ming's acne cleared up and he grew into his head, hands, and feet, but began speaking in his native Mandarin while with the group—an attempt at rebellion that forced him to translate himself or go unheard. Despite their various skin tones, the summer Sun had browned each of them, making them look older than they were.

Pinewood Junior High sat behind its empty parking lot with gloomy abandon. Each step rang a hollow, echoless blast from within the horseshoe building surrounding the walkway. Summer meant no teachers, and any who might have come in would have gone home by now.

"The doors are gonna be locked," Jaden announced with uncertainty.

"I'm surprised there isn't a chain and padlock around the handle," admitted Sam.

"I hope the door's locked," Ming declared hiding his shame in Mandarin.

The boys approached the doors and stopped as if on cue. Their atypical game of *Chicken* electrified the static in the air and each mind raced with unbalanced emotion. Sam stepped forward and reached for the chain-and-padlock-less handles, giving them a hard tug. To all their surprise the doors swung out with ease. Ming, wiping the sweat from his forehead, let out a sigh. Jaden stretched his sweaty fingers away from his palm.

"You guys comin'?" Sam stood in the foyer, grinning from ear to ear.

Ming stepped forward and whispered to himself, "this is a bad idea."

"What's that mean?" Jaden asked, following Ming.

Ming glanced at Jaden and shook his head.

The missing echo from the walkway came back with a vengeance, each sound made by the boys replicating into conflicting vibrations, vibrations destroyed by their own focused reflection. The familiar office windows, hallways, and lockers had been dressed down, stripped of any sign of life. A lone banner hung above the office doors reading: *Welcome To Pinewood Junior High, 1991.* The boys strolled through the halls shouting obscenities, swearing off the teachers they hadn't liked, and slapping any and every surface that caught their attention. Each made a point to visit their first locker, to try their old code.

Each failed.

Once the excitement of their adolescent drive to resist subsided, the reality of their criminal enterprise had begun to set into each of their minds. Jaden didn't want to disappoint his mother, to wind up like his brother. Ming had been working hard to unsettle any chance of blending in but knew that a criminal record was beyond the limits of his rebellion. Sam had already been in hot water at home, resisting her mother's insistence on being more ladylike, and couldn't help but feel she'd be sent to some relative in New England, to be rehabilitated, if the police were to get involved.

"I've gotta piss," Sam announced with pride.

Heading down the hall Jaden realized he'd been directed to Mr. Woodhouse's History class. History had been the only class he earned an A in, and he swore it was Woodhouse's teaching. Sam slapped the wall outside of the boys' bathroom, swinging herself through the open doorway. Ming followed, stopped, and then went into the girls' bathroom instead.

Jaden stood in the empty hall and felt completely alone for the first time. The once massive shafts of lockers and doors had exhaled and constricted. A chill ran up Jaden's spine, jolting his body, and persuading him to visit his old haunt. The door to Mr. Woodhouse's class pulled toward him with an ease he hadn't remembered, only to release the familiar scent of pink erasers, bleach-washed desks, and pencil shavings.

The room had been the same as he remembered, with the map of the world hanging from the front of the class and the overhead projector sitting in the corner. A 49ers flag still hung above the door. Despite the familiarity, the room sat silent, still, and darker than the rest of the school. There had been one source of light in the room, only a small window framing a streetlight. Jaden passed the first row of desks before the click of the closing door startled him.

"Come on," he whispered. "You're fourteen. You can't be getting scared by a door."

The desks passed beside him and the map grew larger and more visible. His eyes passed from Northern Canada to the southernmost point of South America before jumping to South Africa.

A spark erupted in the corner of Jaden's eye, a firefly dancing against the wall. He twisted to watch the luminous bug only to be surprised by its flattened form. The flattened light grew in diameter and brightness, illuminating the room. The once button-sized light grew into a blinding sheet. Jaden stood frozen in awe. The light suddenly shifted revealing a face within the wall behind it. Terror flooded the boy's heart. *It's in the wall,* he thought. The face's dark skin wrinkled as though its soul had outlasted its physical form. Its white eyes housed small, dark pupils which darted around in search of an intruder. Eyes that landed upon Jaden.

The boy could hear himself scream, could feel himself falling to the ground. He was out of control. Before hitting the floor, he watched as the pinkish mouth grew beyond its natural limits revealing long white teeth, laughing at his fear.

The door to the classroom shot open, and Ming and Sam sprinted in, ready to fight.

"What happened?!" Ming shouted in English, breaking his rebellious oath.

"Who's here?" Sam asked, swiveling around in search of a threat.

Jaden couldn't speak, couldn't move. The light had vanished in an instant and the space on the wall had returned to its original state, to a calendar without a face.

"What was it? A rat?" Sam had crouched beside Ming and began inspecting Jaden.

Jaden finally broke his spell; "I-I saw a face."

Ming and Sam looked to each other for affirmation, before looking back to Jaden. The room swelled with vibration, with static from their silence. The clock above the chalkboard struck nine and each of the boys jumped in fright. A burst of light laughter broke the silent streak. The group exited the classroom, Jaden stopping in the doorway and looking back to the wall. No face. No face at all. The boys made their way through the halls and to the main doors. For a moment, inspired by their imaginations, each of them expected them to be locked, for a chain and padlock to be hanging around the handles. To their relief, it wasn't and there weren't.

The Sun had long dipped below the horizon, and the Moon revealed the sky. The sidewalks and streets were devoid of traffic. The world stood still. Jaden, Ming, and Sam interrupted the static and passed through with electricity. Summer was coming to an end.

Snow blanketed the sky and ground only interrupted by the tracks of passing cars and foot traffic. Jaden stepped from the greyhound bus with his backpack and suitcase, unprepared for the snowy cold against his thin shoes and denim jeans. The bus station bustled and buzzed with activity as students were reunited with their families. Jaden felt a burst of sentiment in the air, massaging his heart with its resonance. Ming stood in the small building with a cardboard sign reading "JADE." He wore his smile and matching palm-top beanie.

"Jade?" Jaden asked through a laugh.

"I ran out of space!" Ming winked and stretched his arms wide to hug Jaden.

Despite their short time apart, a certain comfort fell over them.

"So what's the plan?" Jaden asked, setting his suitcase on the ground.

Sam erupted from the crowd with both arms stretched, prepared to embrace Ming and Jaden.

"You gotta wait for me!" Sam shouted as she grabbed the pair in a group hug.

The snow outside had begun to settle, letting the Sun blaze through the sky. The gang stashed their belongings in the trunk of Ming's car before heading back to town. Jaden told stories of his brief time at University, Sam described the openness she felt in Seattle and how she might stay after finishing school, and Ming complained about working for his parents at the family store.

The sky hung a pinkish-orange glow, dense with vapid snowflake agility. The boys were out. They loudly sang along to Coolio, Oasis, and Outkast. The town had undergone much-needed upgrades and glowed with concentrated light, light that trailed across the roof of Ming's car like fingers through hair. They passed the high school, an idea crossing Jaden's mind.

"We should visit Pinewood."

"Why?" Sam asked.

Ming glanced at Jaden with intrigue.

"You guys remember the Summer before freshman year?" A smile stretched across Jaden's face. "How different things probably are from what we remember? I'd bet it looks a whole lot different now than it did then."

"I remember how scared you were that we were gonna get caught," Sam chimed.

"And finding you pale-faced in Woodhouse's classroom," Ming added before glancing at Jaden in the passenger seat.

Jaden's grin faded and he glanced at Sam in the back. The car fell silent, save the low hum of The Smashing Pumpkins.

A sudden jerk brought the car to a stop. Ming looked past Jaden, prompting him and Sam to follow suit, craning their necks toward the passenger windows. Pinewood Junior High stood beside them. Its paint had faded and chipped, subtly marking the passing of time. The howl of wind muted the sound of the car doors closing. The boys shivered inside their coats, vibrating with anxious curiosity.

Pacing the walkway, Sam thought she could see the vague outline of chains hanging from the center of the doors.

"It's probably locked," Jaden guessed.

"No way," Ming confidently rebuked. "You said that last time."

"Yeah, and you were speaking Chinese…"

Approaching the door, Sam and Jaden stopped as if on cue. Ming lunged forward and grabbed the handle, yanked. The door swung out with ease, wafting warm air into the snowy night. The boys entered the darkened corridor. A single column of dimly lit lamps beamed from above, providing just enough light to increase the creep factor. Static filled the space, pressed against each of their chests in anxious anticipation. The familiar office windows, hallways, and lockers had been dressed down, stripped of any sign of life. A lone banner hung above the office doors reading: *Welcome To Pinewood Junior High, 1995.* The building seemed to have gotten smaller in its age, more shallow and frail than they remembered.

"So what now?" Sam barked, interrupting the silence.

"We could go find our lockers," Ming answered.

"Do you remember your locker numbers?" Jaden asked, defeating Ming's plan.

"The cafeteria," Ming announced, beginning his trek before finishing the words.

"Ooh," Sam followed.

Jaden stood in the hallway watching his friends disappear between the narrow columns of light. *Breaking and entering for middle school cafeteria food*, he thought. After peering down the halls, considering his situation, he began in his own direction. The lockers, lining either side of the hall, had been just the same. Seeing them from his new height, Jaden felt a sense of his own growth. The unmanaged mounds of dust that topped each of the aluminum cabinets reminded him of his life, of the clarity that seems to come with adulthood. He breezed past the spaces he hadn't seen before, remnants of unwritten histories, unaware of his route or destination. Passing twin bathroom entrances, Jaden stopped with his feet on a familiar track.

He stood outside of Mr. Woodhouse's classroom and studied the name engraved on the plaque. *He's still teaching here*, Jaden thought. For a brief moment, he felt as though he and the door were the only objects in existence, surrounded by infinite blackness. He watched his hand reach out for the door and pull it toward him. The dark room released the familiar scent of pink erasers, bleach-washed desks, and pencil shavings, luring him in. Passing the threshold of his old haunt, Jaden felt a sense of overwhelming discomfort. The room had been rearranged, now facing the lone window. Quickly scanning, Jaden recognized Woodhouse's desk and *49rs* flag in their rooted spaces. A thick, grey coat of dust obscured the flag's fading face.

"Wow," he heard himself sigh.

Jaden passed the tattered desks, chipped and scratched from decades of abuse. He traced his fingers along the surfaces, studying each and every groove in search of a familiar track. As he reached the front of the room, turning in place, he saw the view his beloved teacher must have seen nearly every day. The room vibrated with unrelenting silence, goosebumps forming on Jaden's neck in anticipation.

Silence.

Without explanation, Jaden sensed a shift in the room against his motionless body. To his right, Woodhouse's desk sat as it always had. Above his foam-dripping office chair, a yellowing Rolodex, and uneven pencils standing in a mug, hung a square, 6-inch calendar with the faces of various retro animated characters. The last date checked was December 15, 1995. *Friday*, Jaden thought, *only a few days ago.* The thought of his relative closeness to his mentor induced a sense of ease within him.

Then he remembered the face. The face that somehow peered through the wall, cursing him with its haunting glance. The same face that visited him in his dreams, left him sleepless for weeks after the event. He hadn't spoken of it and assumed it was his imagination. The no-face wasn't there. It hadn't ever been. Just the wide, uncanny smiles of children's cartoons.

Jaden left the room and passed through the vacant halls, another final exit from his favorite class. The emptiness of the halls fell to the side of his inexplicable disappointment. He'd spent so much time convincing himself he'd only imagined the face, maybe he had imagined it. Maybe he'd only been convincing himself he had seen it. Lost in thought, he was surprised by how quickly he found himself in the cafeteria.

"...and sure enough she took the cat," Sam finished

Ming and Sam sat opposite each other at a lone table, a long stretch untouched beside them. Empty pudding containers littered the space between them.

"Pudding?" Jaden interrupted.

"You think I'm about to cook middle school mac 'n cheese?" Ming answered.

The boys cleaned their mess and drifted back to the building's entrance. For a moment each of them thought they saw chains on the front door, chains that faded as they neared their exit. Snow fell in an unforgiving flurry, covering the tracks of all former life, drawing them back into the world.

Jaden pulled the U-Haul into his driveway. The driveway to his *new* old house. The passing of his late mother resulted in the inheritance of his childhood home and a plethora of forgotten memories. He exited the truck, scanned the old neighborhood, and watched the sun in its familiar place. An autonomous *chirp* dragged its jagged teeth through the air, cutting through the comfort of silence. Jaden pulled his black and grey Motorola from his pocket, flipped it open, and placed it to his ear.

"Welcoming committee," a voice sang.

"Ming," Jaden smiled and turned back to the truck. "Excellent timing."

"I know you probably can't wait to start unpacking, but I'll be there around six to pick you up."

"I-uh," Jaden hesitated. "Yeah. Sure, sounds good."

They finished their brief call and Jaden began transferring boxes from the truck into the garage. Each box that he moved carried the burden of beginning a new career. The cut in his tenure at the college seemed a fair trade for a house outside of urbanity. *His* house. And Fir Ridge Community College *had* offered a surprisingly enticing onboarding package, even if the offer came from a committee of familiar names. He finished the process in an hour with thirty minutes to spare, ten of which were spent digging for a tote labeled *clothes*. Jaden found the replica of his favorite MC Hammer shirt and tossed it to the side with a pair of lesser-abused jeans.

Ming announced his arrival with the goose honk of his Yugo. The same red matchbox he'd been driving since high school. Jaden pulled the door behind him and approached the car sporting an adolescent spring in his step. They greeted and agreed that it was as though time hadn't passed at all, fighting for auditory space with Bloc Party's propelling guitars.

The sky hung a pinkish-orange glow, dense with vapid pollen agility. The boys were out. After sharing a round of drinks, exchanging hyperbolic stories, and forcing down the last of their oversized Mexican dinner plates, Jaden and Ming pulled on their jackets and went for a walk through the streets of Pinewood. They filled the city's evening bustle with laughter and banter, reseating Jaden in his *new* old hometown.

"It's too bad Sam isn't here," Jaden smiled.

"Yeah," Ming sighed. "But she's got a great life in Seattle. She calls me on Sundays and tells me about writing for *The Seattle Times*. A whole lot of politics, I don't care for it, but you know Sam…"

Jaden, steeping in the thought of Sam's new life, suddenly realized where they were. He stopped and turned to the lot on his right. A collection of yellow and black machines mounted the dirt and rubble, skeleton, and structure of the previous construction. Pinewood Middle School. Static filled the air, blanketing any and all sound, while cold fingers wrapped around Jaden's heart.

"I know," Ming broke the static. "It's like a part of our childhood is gone."

"But why?"

"Asbestos. They used to fill buildings with the stuff. My parents just covered the shop in lead paint. Supposed to protect you from it, I guess."

The Old Haunt

Jaden and Ming stood and stared at the remains of the middle school, attempting to map out the nonexistent halls. Halls he had seen for the last time ten years before. Only the walkway, between the deconstructed horseshoe, remained in its original form, albeit covered in dirt. The path to his memories, surrounded by their deconstruction. Memories reduced to memories of memories. The wind turned and a chill pulled them back to reality. Ming and Jaden began their trek back to Ming's car without a word.

Rain fell in an angry percussion, dancing across rooftops and sidewalks. The chilled air picked at Jaden's joints. His fingers tightened around the worn handle of his briefcase as he drudged through the waterlogged parking lot. A barrage of bright yellow, pink, and blue raincoats surrounded and passed him as students ran to the middle school building, splashing him along the way.

Jaden passed through the clinical halls of the building and followed the shining laminated floor. The building reminded him more of the community college than any middle school he'd been to, but his reference points were limited. The building was nothing like Pinewood Middle School and had none of the adolescent electricity he could remember. Or, he'd wondered, was that just his imagination? Was he only opining the brilliance of a long-gone past? Regardless, it was only a structure. Any residual emotion he might be remembering would have certainly outlasted the old school's deconstruction and would linger on amidst the current halls. At least, that's what the movies say. His regular route led him to his classroom. On top of his desk, beside his keyboard and mouse, stood a photo in a frame; three young specters with smiles pulled across their faces. He glanced at the photo and smiled, missed his late friend, and looked forward to his weekly call with Sam on Sunday.

Slowly, a trickle of young teens spilled into the room and filled the emptiness. Their chatter, occasionally rising above his preferred volume, generated a buzz that filled the room, and pushed gently against his chest. For a moment the room seemed to be reverberating the electricity from his childhood. A smile stretched across his wrinkled face, displaying his perfectly human teeth.

"All right," Jaden began, "let's see who's here."

Jaden took attendance, subtly mispronouncing the easier names to cover for the harder ones. He'd learned this technique teaching at the college and found that it made him appear less intimidating if he made a harmless mistake on the first day, without singling anyone else out.

"And I," Jaden started, "am Mr. Knowles. I'll be your seventh-grade homeroom teacher, so please feel free to come to me with any questions you might have. I know middle school is a big change and can be scary, I was in your place once. I went to school here. Well, not *here* at New Channel, but the school that was here before it, Pinewood."

Jaden repeated this process for four other classes, introducing himself and mispronouncing the easy names. The buzz he felt in his first-period class resonated, only dimming during the third period, his lunch break. The final bell rang and students flooded the halls with stories of their first day, rumors of kindling crushes, and haphazard plans to carpool home. Jaden listened to the roar, smiling as he collected his day's materials. The roar blazed before settling to a hum, and finally, the school was filled with near silence.

Walking to his car, Jaden saw that the clouds and rain had slowly retreated through the day, shining hope on his new position at the school. He passed through the staggered parking lot, and briefly watched as unknown members of the faculty carelessly packed into their cars and trickled away. Arriving at his gunmetal Prius, a realization occurred. He'd forgotten the charger for his laptop, the only one he had. Slipping his briefcase into the passenger seat of his car, Jaden closed the door and headed back to the building, fingering his employee badge on the way.

Slipping in and out of the classroom with his charger, he waited for the resonance to press against him as it had before. He felt nothing. The halls were free of any fluctuations save the sound of his soles against the cold, laminated floor. Jaden stopped in the hall. Swiveling his head, he began to consider his position in accordance with the old school. The current floor plan had little resemblance to the original, but he realized he'd been near Woodhouse's old classroom.

To his delight, a door stood in the very same position as Woodhouse's door. Jaden pulled it open revealing a dark supply closet. Slipping his phone from his pocket, he shined the flashlight into the room and saw the impossible. Beyond the mops, buckets, and chemicals stood a familiar classroom. *Woodhouse's classroom.* The old haunt. Suddenly, Jaden noticed the small figure standing before him; a young, dark-skinned boy in an MC Hammer shirt. The boy fell to the floor and let out a scream. Just as he opened his mouth, a bell announced that the building would be locked, startling Jaden. Looking back into the closet he saw a gray wall behind the mops and buckets.

The sky hung a pinkish-orange glow, dense with brisk clarity. Jaden was out. He left the school with an adolescent spring in his step. The wind breezed through his open windows as he drove through town, singing along to Bouncing House. The glowing city lights blazed across the sky, soaking the windshield and combing the roof of his car.

Hiroshige, *Yui*

—16th station in 53 Stations of the Tōkaidō, *1831–34*

Ricardo Pau-Llosa

It is never our intent to ambush the real,
let alone the beautiful or frightening, from the edges
we assign to ourselves. We accuse the craggy trail,
the piling inevitables that drift us onto ridges

from which finality drops us in the midst of awe.
Surely, we could not gasp at sea and mountain,
nor see the neat sails as symbols of our art
within our art, if courage loosed but villain

pure had not dangled us brash and free.
Is it courage: the vulture's drunken height,
the naked trunk roped by wind yet tree
enough to root on starving rock? If not,

what compels beyond the grip of sanity
to hoard the world in a blink and scold serenity?

I am the shadow sister of Icarus

Diane Averill

living in the dark corners of my father's life,
watcher of obsession
while my father Daedalus
with that brilliant, twisted mind
became architect of the labyrinth
enclosing the Minotaur

half human, half bull, a strong son
who grew too wild for him to control,
charging through the maze
with a mind crazed as my father's stubborn pride.

Icarus, never loved
in his own right
but only as a reflection of our father
struggled with the wax wings Daedalus placed
on his shoulders.

They took off towards the sun
leaving me to light the empty room
out of the tallow I made my own wings.

I am the shadow sister of Icarus

My flight began that night—
the breezes, sudden gusts of wind,
riding the thermals as temperatures rose
flying high, then higher
under the moon
and her eight changing moods
then dipping down over the blue-gray ocean
its ecstatic waves echoed by gulls.

Bruegel didn't paint me
as he did when my brother's wings melted
in the too-high flight under a blazing sun,
his tragic fall into unforgiving waters
unnoticed by everyone,
yet the painting made Icarus
forever famous

while I, Luna, flew on into the years,
landing only on my own terms
an old woman now
crafting the round cedar home
in a wildflower meadow
and watching the birds swoop down
as I tell you my story.

After Life

Nathan Bas

I hear them through the window
moving out the house in 3 years
as my hallway absorbs a part of me
to haunt the new owners once I die

                              long from now

the 42 blueberry bushes in the back swim
with the weeds and the rot spreading to each corner; fenced
as a property moving to a new owner and age
without the shovel that brought it out of the old

all manicured by hired helpers
their retirement home will never be more
than a place of deceased history
never jogging the torch back into place—
chained like a tortured lapdog

After Life

—I'll mourn old joints lost in memory
moving back through the various plantings
cutting-downs
to the cries of their birth

                              and mine

Anticipation

Lawrence F. Farrar

Comfortable behind the wheel of his Mercedes, Blake Matthews stayed alert for the off-ramp that would lead him to Riverton and, he hoped, to Molly Chandler. He'd confirmed she still lived there with a white pages' search. Blake had come this way before, but each time his resolve had dissipated. Now, he was determined. The years were ebbing away.

Outfitted in chinos, a plaid shirt, and fall jacket, Blake was a sixty-five-year-old widower. A former academic (East Asian history), he had a high nose (his deceased wife had declared it Patrician) and gray eyes. His still plentiful hair, too, was gray. He thought of his appearance as distinguished. Perhaps. But facial folds and creases underscored the fact his youth was long gone. Vanity condemned his wire-framed glasses to a shirt pocket.

Blake hoped to find Molly at home. Leaving the highway, he brimmed with anticipation. He so wanted to see her--sweet, wonderful Molly. He'd long ago reconciled himself to losing her (or so he told himself). Still, the question that dogged him all these years persisted. Why? Why had she turned away? The laceration had never healed.

Driving down Main Street, Blake saw Riverton much as he remembered it. Brick-fronted shops and business and a grid of modest one-story houses. It was a place where farmers swapped stories at the Blue Fox Café on Saturday morning, where American Legionnaires marched to the Union Cemetery on Memorial Day, where Lion Club members roared, and Rotarians performed civic works. A good place to grow up—everybody agreed. But, at twenty, Blake had wanted to be free of the town, especially once Molly broke his heart.

Blake parked his car at Riverside Park. He needed to think more about what he would say to her. How would she react? Seated on a bench, he felt the sharp bite of autumn. Cardinals, wrens, and warblers created a tapestry of chirping and whistling. Squirrels scurried about. How often had he and Molly cuddled on one of these benches watching the night-time river glide by? Awash in the past, it seemed he'd never left. Logic, of course, warned him otherwise. The past existed as a clutch of truncated oddments, soon to be obliterated. But, like a pilgrim seeking something soul affirming, he resisted that reality. Instead, he clutched at the memories lest they slip away altogether.

Twenty minutes later, Blake slid into a booth in Bailey's Coffee Shop. He relished the sound and sweet smell of wood crackling in a raised fireplace. Molly's phone number in hand, he permitted his mind to explore possibilities. A curative word, perhaps even a curative touch. Did she harbor a hidden story, one waiting to be heard? The prospect of finally solving the mystery that resurrected itself with soul-destroying frequency encouraged him. Yet, apprehension shadowed the anticipation that animated him. The possibility of a bad outcome thrust itself upon him.

Nonetheless, he mustered his resolve and called her on his cell.

"Hello." Her voice sounded so familiar, as if he'd just spoken to her the day before.

"Molly? This is Blake. Blake Matthews."

For a moment, she made no response.

"Blake? Is it really you?" She searched for words. "Where are you? Why are you calling?" Hardly the enthusiastic response he'd envisioned. Still, a frisson of excitement surged through him.

"On my way to a Chicago. Saw the turn-off. Couldn't resist. I hoped we might have a chance to talk."

"Oh, I don't think that..."

"Maybe I could swing by your house."

More silence. "No. I don't think that would be a good idea," she said. She seemed distant.

"How about meeting me here? It's called Bailey's."

"It's been so many years. Do you think there is any point in...?"

"For old time's sake, Molly. Just for a half hour or so. For old time's sake."

He waited an eternal minute.

Finally, she said, "Alright. It's one o'clock. I'll meet you there at two."

"Great, Molly," he said, his voice buoyant. "Great. I'll see you then." She had already hung up.

Blake attempted a grilled-cheese sandwich, worked through two cups of coffee, made a trip to the restroom, and browsed a copy of the *River Times*. He checked the obituaries; nobody he knew.

Mostly he tried to ready his mind for the appearance of a sixty-something Molly. But he could only picture the twenty-year-old Molly. Preternaturally bright, she'd been so full of laughter. Like a flower in the morning sun, she'd been especially pretty, especially desirable. Her dark eyes had allured him; her long dark hair had allured him. He remembered her hands, slender and sensitive, gliding across the piano keys.

He had loved her beyond all imagining. And she'd told him she loved him, too. What of the all-consuming emotions? What of the all-consuming seizures of desire? Had she rejected all of it? He surely had not. Why had she turned away? So cruelly? So out of character? Why the letter of abrupt rejection that reached him at Tan Son Nhut? He'd repeatedly tried to contact her, his letters and calls unheeded. In the end, he'd surrendered to a crushing reality—she'd abandoned him.

Now he looked up and saw her at the entrance. She shaded her eyes with a hand, as she searched the room. He'd feared she might appear worn out by life, but, although dimmed, her confidence and beauty still showed through. She possessed a familiar elegance. Her black hair, gone to gray, was now short and well organized. She wore a cardigan, a blouse and a skirt, all age appropriate. Blake's feelings jittered. He'd not expected so much emotion.

As she approached, he rose to his feet. "It's good to see you, Molly. Very good."

He thought to embrace her. But she pre-empted him by extending her hand. "Hi, Blake. It's nice to see you, too. How many years has it been?" Her voice was soft, but firm.

"More than forty, I guess."

They slid into a booth and faced each other. She sat erect, hands folded in her lap, like someone at an uncomfortable job interview.

"Would you like coffee?" Blake said.

"Yes, just coffee."

A waitress took their orders. Neither spoke until she left.

"You look good, Blake. I've heard you've had a fine life. Big-time correspondent or such. Even a professor?"

"Yes, it's gone pretty well for me." What did she know of his life? What sorts of things had she heard? Did she ever think of him, as he did of her?

"How about you, Molly? How are you doing?"

"Fine, just fine." She looked down and brushed an invisible speck of lint from her sleeve.

They again stopped talking when the waitress delivered their order.

"Tell me about yourself, Blake said." He wanted to sweep away the formalities, the nugacities. He wanted to ask her straight away, why she had rid herself of him? Tossed him away like an old shirt. Why?

"I heard a long time ago you were widowed," Blake said. He wished he had not raised that yet. He'd wondered if her husband been the one responsible for their breakup.

"Yes; it was years ago. You wouldn't have known him. He was not from here."

"You never left?" Blake asked.

"No. I thought of it. But I guess things just didn't work out." He detected a whisper of wistfulness in her words. "Not a world traveler like you, Blake."

"Oh, I'm still the same guy, I..."

She looked at him wryly. "I've had a very ordinary life here in this little town." She gently cleared her throat. "But I get by. It's enough."

Getting by? What did that mean? She seemed to be hiding reality from him. He'd driven by her house. It was a boxy cottage, in need of paint, and with an ill-kept yard. Assuredly, she had not prospered.

"Enough?" His voice took on an edge.

"Yes, Blake. Enough. I have my house. My books. My garden. My cat."

Her cat? He'd forgotten the cats.

"Are you well?" he said. "We're getting older."

"Yes, I'm well." He supposed he could expect no other reply.

"It might have been different, Molly. It might have been different."

He sought to give meaning to her responsive smile. Did they, in fact, share an unspoken, unrealized dream? Or was it simply kindness?

They chatted on for five minutes. She mentioned a few old friends. Recalled a favorite teacher. But never did she address the issue most on Blakes's mind.

He could wait no longer. "Molly. Why? Why did you turn away?"

She again busied herself with the invisible lint. "Haven't we talked enough about the old days?" She avoided his eyes.

"But, Molly, you can at least tell me..."

Head bent and meditative, she said, "Whatever happened was for the best."

"Perhaps so, but I still don't know..."

She raised her head and cleared her throat again. "Blake, please. We can't relive what's gone. That's all there is to it."

"I wish it was that simple, but..."

An extended silence came between them. She seemed detached, almost a stranger, which in a way he supposed she had become.

Finally, she spoke, her voice saturated with resignation. "Things are what they are, Blake."

Was it a pose? Was she concealing something?

"Was it your mother? I don't think she liked me."

"Oh, Blake, why do you say that? Mom liked you. So did my dad." She stifled a smile, as if it were a silly question.

"Is there something I should know? Something that's hard to say?"

She slowly shook her head.

Had she begun to open up, even a little? Blake seized the opportunity.

"Was there a child?" He blurted it out. He had long wrestled with the possibility.

"I've had no child. Would it have mattered?"

Her answer perplexed him. "Of course, it would have mattered," he said. In those days, pregnant and unwed could seem to mean ruin.

She failed to revisit the question; offered no further clarification. "It would have been better if we hadn't met today." She retrieved a handkerchief from a small purse and dabbed at her eyes.

Her non-response depressed Blake. His inability to elicit an answer depressed him more.

"I'd should go now," Molly said. "I think it's best if you don't contact me again." She lowered her eyes as manifest sadness transited her face.

He'd craved an unambiguous answer but found none. Nothing had changed. Perhaps it was better he *not* know. At least, he could then conjure an answer that satisfied him.

Molly slid out of the booth. "Goodbye, Blake. Good luck with the rest of your life. It was nice of you to think of me." She delivered a life-is-like-that smile, marched to the door, and went out.

Two untouched cups of coffee remained on the table.

Blake lingered a while longer, thinking. You anticipated things, built up your hopes. It felt good. But then things didn't work out, and the anticipation proved unfounded. The people we left behind evaporated. They existed only in fragmented memories, imprecise, shadowed figures of our imagination. Time had moved on without him; people had moved on without him; and Molly had moved on without him. Blake knew it. But he did not want to accept it.

The day would amount to nothing more than a snapshot in time, blurred and soon deleted. Even so, he drove to Molly's house and parked across the street. Perhaps he could try once more. Just walk up and knock on the door. He sat in the car for five minutes, took a deep breath, and pulled away.

Looking for America

Steve Deutsch

Let us be
best friends
one last time—

roll out the old
Ford
and take

that trip
we so often
dreamed of

when young.
Head to
the west coast

on those two lane
roads that once
were America.

Remember
when we were
America too?

Fill that old
Ford with
chips and beer—

the radio set
to the "Nothing
but Oldies" Station,

loud enough
to remind us
we are still alive.

Swap lies
with the locals
in pubs on Main Street

and sample
the biscuits and bacon
in dozens of mom

and pop diners
in what was once
the heartland—

Looking for America

a thousand dots
on a tattered
gas station map

long ago
bypassed
and nearly forgotten.

And when
the Ford
throws a rod

in Kansas
or Colorado,
as of course

it must,
we can unfold
the aluminum

lawn chairs
and sit on the berm
to wait for the sunset.

The Cartographers

Nate Maxson

Every London taxi driver
Has to take a grueling exam
On the layout of the city
They have to know and memorize every street
Inside out
And they refer to this test
As, "The Knowledge"
They drive out into the city on motorbikes
To practice planning routes
It can take years until they're ready

I think I should make it clear that I've never been to London
And can't name any of its streets
Except probably some of the ones reserved for tourists
But sometimes I do daydream,
The fleets of young mapmakers zipping nimbly,
Endlessly rediscovering
Hidden cities busy with the act of hiding
Houdinilike cities,
Paths drawn in ink on their forearms
Explorations and intrusions, I've heard the rain never stops
Over bridges and rivers and concrete tunnels

The Mercator Projection
If you believed the map
You would assume
Antarctica went on forever

Steven

Paul Willis

...that best portion of a good man's life,
His little, nameless, unremembered acts
Of kindness and of love.

                —Wordsworth, *"Tintern Abbey"*

We assumed by Christmas it would come—
the letter with the promised news of grief.
Columbus Day had brought the doctor's word
of fresh discoveries within the spine,
dark islands in that archipelago.
Thanksgiving brought no hope of anything
for which to give our thanks. He understood
the end was near, and wrote to say his wife
would tell us when his voyage had reached its verge.

To tell you what that meant I'll have to say
what he had meant to us. So. Have you seen
still waters before dawn upon a lake
high up in the Sierra, say a mile
away from the dust-trampled John Muir Trail—
the calmness of the surface that before
was tossed by winds and torn by thunderstorms?

Steven

And have you felt the silence on the shore—
cool silence where, before, mosquitoes plagued
the tangled net that drooped about your head?
He was like that—the one you wanted in
your life to calm and cool what troubled you,
someone with depths reflective of the dawn.
We were the travelers; he was always there,
the place to visit, place to say we would
return to when we could—a lake, I say,
that always shines beneath the morning star.
Of course, that is not possible: the winds
will come, mosquitoes will return. But there
was something in his eye, his smile, which said
that such a place existed in his soul—
and we might share it. That is what he meant
upon our meeting him beside the trail.

We were a pair of hikers, fast intent
on making it from Mexico across
the desert to the High Sierra on
that slender way, then through the Siskiyous, up
the long volcanic backbone of the range
still known as the Cascades—as yet unknown
to us. Amanda was from Michigan,
and I from Illinois. We'd met in college,
married, wondered what was next for us.
She'd gotten tired of managing the deli,
I of applying to graduate school, and so
we thought, why not? Before we're too tied down,

Steven

let's take a trip to hold within our hearts
when we're too frail to step without a cane.
We'd heard of a new trail along the crest
of the Pacific, where we'd never been,
had read a book by a young man who said
he'd walked from Canada to Mexico.
That first part sounded icy in the spring,
so we decided we'd go south-to-north.
That boy was Eric Ryback. Later he
was proved to be a fraud by an old man
who drove a log truck on the dusty roads
beneath Mt. Shasta, gave the boy a ride
before he could think better and decline.
This was years before that Cheryl Strayed
would make the trail famous by her strange
and partial walk. But still, the mountain path
was gaining visitors, and we in truth
were not much more prepared or apt than she
when we arrived in California.

That first part of the hike was nothing much,
a prairie without grass, bare lonely plains,
with miles between sad springs. And we were new
to pack straps digging deep, the ache of hips
and shoulders underneath our heavy loads.
Too heavy—at the first small crossroads we
unloaded half my books, the frying pan,
and left our camp chairs in a vacant shack.

Steven

The month was April, warm by afternoon,
but cool at night—we kept our goose-down bags.

The blisters came before we reached the hills,
big gaping sores upon our toes and heels.
They almost did us in; we limped in pain
and wondered how two thousand miles and more
could possibly undo our throbbing wounds.
But tape and bandages eventually
turned sores to callouses, and our stiff boots
began to soften, mile by tender mile.
And by the time we reached Tehachapi,
our feet were sturdy instruments that clocked
each stretch of trail like steady metronomes.

There had been spring snowstorms on San Jacinto,
and snowbanks on the flanks of San Gorgonio,
but nothing quite prepared us for the width
and depth of snowpack in the true Sierra.
Past Kennedy Meadows, we climbed into winter,
even though the calendar said June.
And suncups—had we even heard of such?
We stumbled through declivities hip-deep—
hard in the morning, mush in afternoon—
and stepped and fell, and stepped and fell again.
Ants in egg cartons, drunks inside a maze—
that's what we felt like, that is all we were.

So, when at last we got to Cottonwood,
we hitched the road to Lone Pine in defeat.
That's when we met him, sitting at a turn,
cross-legged, pack beside him, in the sun.
We'd yet to find a ride—there hardly was
a car or truck that passed—but, far below,
the empty shimmer of broad Owens Lake
stretched out across the desert, welcome mat
to, yes, Death Valley just a glimpse beyond.
He raised his hand in greeting. "Headed down?
Me too. That snow..." He nodded up the road.
"We're tired of it too," Amanda said.
We had seen no one for three days and more;
the lilt within her voice told me how glad
we were for company, though three of us
decreased our chances of a lift to town.
He stood and yawned. "I'm Steve," he simply said.
"Or Steven—don't go in for trail names
like Esker, Desperado, Evening Song.
No need to hide our true identities."
We introduced ourselves, and just like that
a pickup came around the curve and stopped.
We clambered in, all three, and felt the wind
warm in our faces as it shifted low
down switchbacks to the Alabama Hills.

And then the streets of Lone Pine. We got out,
Mt. Whitney hovering above us now,
and Steven said, "Some breakfast? I can buy."

Steven

How strange to hear the clink of knives and forks
within a restaurant, to be indoors.
A waitress poured us coffee, offered eggs.
"You've had some sun," she said. "Just rest a bit."
I had five pancakes, sausages, as much
of orange juice as anyone could hold.
And then we talked, and talked, and talked some more.
He was from Oregon, always wanted to
link up the Skyline Trail with what led south.
Somehow, he'd made it through the streams and snow
en route to Mexico. "You'll need," he said,
"two pair of crampons to resume your way.
You can have mine—I'll do without, the snow
won't last so long for me—the other you
can get somewhere in town. Ice axes too—
old long ones, wooden shafts, to bring you through
the suncups while they last. Don't bother with
the crooked kind—you won't be climbing ice.
Just plug along, eat watermelon snow,
and watch the rosy finches hop from crest
to crest. Soon you will do the same. Soon you
will glide from pass to pass as if with wings."
We looked at him. "You sure?" He winked, pulled back.
"Just think pure thoughts," he said, "and you will fly."
I laughed. But not Amanda. She was willing
to take his word for gospel, I could tell.

And so, we found our axes, rented spikes
to strap beneath her boots, and soon all three

of us were hitching back to Cottonwood.
We parted ways—we north, he south—and hugged
spontaneously at the trailhead.
And he was right—we flew across the snows
like hungry swallows, stopping in the vales
to peck out campsites on sweet spots of ground.
Before we knew it, we were past the worst.
Or best, I should say, all that shining crest
of Langley, Russell, Forester, LeConte—
then Evolution, Mono, Silver Pass,
the Postpile, Agnew, Thousand Island Lake,
Tuolumne, and on to Tower Peak,
that northern boundary of Yosemite.
Then Tahoe, Lassen, Shasta, Sisters, Hood;
Rainier and Glacier, Baker to the west;
at last across Pasayten Wilderness
among the burning larches in the fall
to Manning Park in Canada, our goal.
At each small post office along the way,
a plain postcard from Steven: "Almost there!
You've got it made! Your feet are singing now—
your feet are singing in full harmony!"

Sometimes, at evening in a northern meadow,
the pikas squeaking, marmots whistling clear,
we'd speak of him, and wonder at his presence
that lasted long beyond the day we'd met.
"It's not that I'm in love," Amanda'd say—
"with him, I mean. It's just that he loved us.

So unaccountably. That's just the thing.
He didn't have to help us, but he did."

We keep those crampons that he gave to me
upon the mantel, like some crown of thorns.
When our kids ask about them, we just say,
"They got us through—a gift from a dear friend."
They're rusty now, the leather straps are worn,
the points are dulled—just like my thinking when
I've graded stacks of papers late at night.
But when I'm tempted to write something cruel
within the margins of a freshman theme,
I think of Steven, pancakes, and a smile
that helped us live our dreams and graduate
to this our life we take such pleasure in.
No more than that—a small assist, a little
gesture (large in retrospect), a way
of being, like a lake new-freed from ice—
no wind, no bugs, the clear and morning star.

Mr. Stream

Dean Engle

The Museum for the Umpqua River Light is secretly one of the saddest places I've ever been. The museum itself is beautiful, an old, Cape Cod style building, all white paint and wind shutters, protected from the elements by a line of majestic cypress trees. It is just the history that is sad. Inside, as with nearly all museums, it is full of plaques, artifacts, models, and recreations. It's where the tour starts.

It costs eight dollars for a tour, but it's the only way to see the lighthouse. I dutifully pay and am told to wait in the lobby. A minute later, an older man with a long drooping moustache and knit hat made to resemble human hair, greets me with a jocular. "How you doing pal? Follow me!"

I follow him outside across the lot and past the scenic whale watching viewpoint. It is so fogged in, I can't see the ocean, let alone any whales. The tour guide gestures to a whale's jawbone on display. "When I first got here, I thought that was driftwood. Almost got my chainsaw before the boss told me it was whale."

He leads me into the lighthouse itself and shows me the old pictures of the keepers. They all are wearing smocks that look like Ebenezer Scrooge style nightgowns. "They had to wear special smocks while cleaning the lens so they couldn't scratch it. Can't have a scratched light."

He takes me to the stairs next. "They're free standing," he says. "From Portland Ironworks. Stairs like this expand in the heat.

Contract in the cold. If they were attached, they'd pull the bricks off."

The stairs are steep and winding and by the time we make it to the top, the guide is out of breath. He motions for me to take a few steps up, inside the lens.

It is the brightest, largest, best kaleidoscope I have ever seen. Light shimmers through the glass, red diamonds twisting slowly, around and around. It is the single most beautiful man-made thing I've come across. The glass work, the light, even just the geometry of it all, shines in my head. I start to reach for my camera, but a picture could never do it justice.

We walk back down the stairs and the across the lot to the museum. "Take a look around," he tells me. "It's included in the tour."

So I do. The museum talks about the lighthouse, the coast guard station nearby, and the early history of Winchester Bay and Reedsport. Two plaques caught my eye. The first told the story of the first lighthouse.

The Umpqua River Light was the first lighthouse built on the Oregon coast. It was constructed near the mouth of the river. They built it in a strange place. The river runs into the sea, and forms an area of brackish water, not quite river and not quite ocean. All the while wind and erosion created miles and miles of sand dunes, rising in high yellow hills. The fog is often thick. So thick it's nearly impossible to see. Hence the lighthouse.

The area would flood often. And strong winds would buffet the lighthouse, already on weakened shifting ground. In 1863, after only five years of service the lighthouse collapsed. A new lighthouse was built nearly thirty years later on the buffs above the river, where flooding would not be an issue and the ground was firmer.

The second plaque that caught my interest was this. A list of lighthouse keepers for the second lighthouse.

Rasmus Peterson. 1893–94. (Transferred).

Marinus H. Stream. 1894–1896. (Drowned).

Isaac L. Smith. 1896–1898. (Transferred).

I know it's wrong, but I can't help chuckling a little. You have a man whose name contains both the words Stream and Marine, who becomes a lighthouse keeper and then drowns. It is so ironic. So bitterly ironic.

And then I see the next plaque. It is about the weather in the area, and it ends with the story of Marinus Stream. As keeper he was responsible for noting the weather each day. His log ends in a different handwriting. His wife wrote in 1896. "Mr. Stream drowned at 1 p.m. He had gone out on a rescue."

I don't know what part of that quote breaks my heart. Maybe it's the simplicity of it. Two quick, simple sentences. Maybe it's the formality, calling her husband Mr. Stream. Maybe it's just the image of his widow, the day her husband dies, finishing the last line in the logbook, and closing it forever. Or maybe, that he died on a rescue. I can only guess all hands were lost at sea.

I leave the museum sobered. The fog has lifted a little. So, I cross again to the whale watching area. I can see past the fog, past the dunes, past the river, to the ocean thundering in the distance. Behind me the lighthouse's beacon turns, its red light flashing every two seconds.

from *A Week on the Concord & Merrimack Rivers*
—H. D. *Thoreau, 1849*

Peter J. Grieco

Six miles above Amoskeag just before sunset
one of us landed to look for where we could
ask for stores—while the other tested
the opposite shore for a safe spot
to harbor our boat. The first voyager returned
with a flaxen-haired boy whose sparkling eyes
were keen to examine us & the furniture
of our vessel. He pulled us by the hand, home
to meet his pa, who treated us to bread & musk
& water-melon. As we ate on the banks, clear light
fell on the eastern trees & was reflected
in the river, & time held still, in moments
that seemed to consecrate all the history
of which we have read, as being no more
than a faint memory of what is happening
now—leaving us to feel this world is but a canvas
to our imaginations & that our circumstances
come easily in answer to our expectations
& to the demands of our natures. There is only
so much I can accomplish ere health & strength
are gone, & yet it suffices. The bird sits now

just beyond gunshot. I am no piece of crockery

that cannot be jostled; rather, I am

one of those old wooden trenchers,

which first stands at the head of the table,

& at another period makes a milking stool,

& at another is a seat for children,

& does not die till it is well worn out.

Ms. Love and the Plate of Dumplings

An American Expat Exchanges Food with a Turkish Neighbor

Pier Roberts

When I first told my husband that I'd broken Ms. Love's plate, he didn't understand. "Our neighbor?" I said. "You know, the one who brings us food all the time?"

Kenan finally understood when he saw the shards of broken glass in my hands, and then he replied with a pressing question of his own: "Were you able to save the *mantı?*"

I shook my head no, and in the midst of feeling clumsy and guilty, I, too, deeply felt the loss of the *mantı*—a delectable Turkish dish consisting of ground-lamb-filled dumplings covered in a spicy garlic yogurt sauce. We'd both had a taste of Ms. Love's *mantı* before I'd put it in the fridge, and we'd both declared it the best *mantı* we'd ever eaten. I'd tried to make *mantı* once, carefully following a recipe from *The Sultan's Kitchen* cookbook that demanded I knead the dough for eight to ten minutes and then, after letting the *dough* rest, roll it out to a 22-inch circle about a sixteenth of an inch thick. The *mantı* was edible, just barely, but my arms hurt for three days afterward, and I never tried it again.

I call my neighbor Ms. Love because in Turkish her name is Sevgi Hanım, which translates literally to Ms. Love or Ms. Affection. Although her name might sound like the September Playmate of the Month to Americans, Ms. Love is a highly respectable, middle-aged Turkish housewife. Her name is nothing unusual in Turkey, where girls are often given names such as Love, Kindness, Sweet Voice, Pretty Face, or One Thousand Roses, and boys can easily be called Victorious, Triumph, Conqueror, War, and, sometimes, Peace. When I began making friends in Turkey, I quickly realized that learning the English meaning of my friends' names was a surefire way to improve my Turkish vocabulary.

The day we moved into our new apartment, Ms. Love, her husband, Mr. Strong, and their ten-year old daughter, Essential, knocked on the door and presented me and Kenan with a three-course meal beautifully presented on an elegant tray as a welcoming gift. I had a vague memory of my mother doing something similar in the '70s (albeit with a bucket of KFC), and I thought the gesture both quaint and kind. When I recounted the story to a Turkish friend, she asked me what I'd given Ms. Love when I returned her tray and dishes. "Um… clean plates," I said.

"Oh no!" my friend Aylin—English translation Moon Halo— exclaimed. "She'll probably forgive you because you're a foreigner. But in Turkey when a neighbor brings you food, you must prepare food of your own and present it to her when you return her plates."

Oh.

Ms. Love truly is…lovely, and she must have forgiven me immediately because a week later she showed up at my door with a plate of *içli kofte*—sensitive meatballs. *Içli kofte* is a beautiful package of a meatball consisting of savory meat, onions, and spices inside of a rich bulgur/tomato/spice-infused dough. It's considered one the most difficult and delicious foods in Turkish cuisine and is especially famous in Adana, where I live.

Thanks to Aylin, I now knew the rules of the game, and I understood that it was my turn to prepare something special for Ms. Love.

But what in the world could I make?

"Prepare a typical American dish. Show off your favorite American food!" my Turkish friends advised me.

Following this sage yet simple advice wasn't so easy, though. What is a typical American dish? Whenever anyone in Turkey asks me what my favorite American food is, I always say, "Mexican food!" And what is the quintessential American food? Macaroni and cheese? Mashed potatoes and gravy? Apple pie? Meatloaf?

After much thought I finally decided on the simple, very American, and very delicious chocolate chip cookie. First I had to call a friend and ask a couple questions.

"Can something sweet be given in return for a savory?"

"Yes."

"Turkish people eat cookies, don't they?"

"Yes."

There are, predictably, no chocolate chips in Turkey, but I found that by chopping a few chocolate bars into pieces, I could substitute chocolate clumps for chips ("Here, please have some of my chocolate clump cookies!") and nothing much was lost. In fact, the lack of uniformity in the chocolate clumps added a unique texture and a bit of a surprise to an otherwise ordinary, though yummy, cookie.

My life in Turkey as an expat has had its moments of unparalleled splendor and awe, such as when I visited the Aya Sofya in Istanbul for the first time or hiked through a pink valley of rock-carved churches in Cappadocia. There's much that I love about Turkish people and culture: the genuine hospitality; the cup of tea offered wherever you go; stern faces that can so easily break out into raucous laughter; the important role of family and friends.

But this exchanging of food between neighbors can quickly get on a person's nerves. I mean, how many special dishes can a woman have? How much time can a woman find to cook meals for her neighbors? I work full-time and my husband works full-time. One of the perks of our university jobs is that for about $1.50 a day, we get a very adequate and healthy hot lunch served in the university cafeteria on exquisite white china. Monday through Friday that's our main meal, and we whip up something light and easy for dinner, packaged soup, for instance. Generally, I have nothing against cooking, and I consider myself to be a pretty good cook. But every day? Who has time for that?

Ms. Love does.

I mentioned that she's a housewife but let me clarify. Ms. Love is a professional Turkish housewife, by which I mean that she spends almost every second of every day making sure that everything in her house is perfect, not a single speck of dust or dirt anywhere. Nothing is out of place, and most importantly, every meal she cooks is the most incredible, mouthwatering dish you've ever eaten. It hurts me to say this, but it's a simple truth: the typical Turkish housewife, by comparison, makes the average American woman look a bit sloppy in terms of cooking and cleaning.

When I realized that there was no way I could compete with Ms. Love, she began to feed into my domestic insecurities, and I started to fear the ring of the doorbell, afraid to find her there, Betty Crocker-like, plate or tray in hand.

It was around that time that I broke her plate.

Again I turned to my Turkish friends to ask how to proceed. The plate I'd innocently let slip from my hands was an odd sort of piece, not something I could easily replace at the local equivalent of Pottery Barn, and I hoped and prayed that it hadn't belonged to some highly valued set. My friends assured me that no one, not even Ms. Love, would bring food to a neighbor on a valuable plate. They suggested that I buy Ms. Love a replacement plate, something nice, and make a very special dish of something for her. I could explain my accidental clumsiness as I presented the food and the replacement plate to her at the same time.

Salvation, my closest Turkish friend, told me to be sure to buy a replacement plate that I liked myself because, "It would be extremely rude if your neighbor accepted the replacement plate that you offer her. But, of course, you must offer it, and she must see that it's brand new."

"Got it," I said, "sort of."

And then I was left wondering what food to make. I'd already made Ms. Love chocolate chip cookies, my grandma's fried chicken, pumpkin pie at the New Year, lasagna, Spanish tortilla, Indonesian rice. She'd yet to repeat a dish on me, so I didn't feel that I could do so either. Peaches were in season and they were some of the best peaches I'd ever eaten, so after a little thought, I settled on peach cobbler. The smell wafted through the apartment as it cooked, and when it emerged from the oven, it was a work of art: the peaches not too soft, not too hard; the biscuit topping perfectly golden, delectable.

As it turned out, Salvation was right. When I offered Ms. Love the replacement plate and apologized for the unfortunate demise of her plate, she protested vociferously. "No. No. No. I cannot accept this plate! The dessert of course I'll take. Wait one minute. I just made some fresh pastries." She went to her kitchen, where she transferred the peach cobbler to a plate of her own, quickly washed the replacement plate, wiped it dry, and filled it with some unbelievably gorgeous fresh pastries that she'd just, I swear it, not three minutes before taken from the oven.

"Here," she said, "you keep the plate."

I returned home, my plate now full of Ms. Love's pastries, and offered some to Kenan. "She wouldn't accept the plate," I said and fell onto the couch, exhausted from the ordeal. "At least," I sighed, "I don't have a plate of hers I need to return with more special food on it."

"Not for now," he said as he bit into one of Ms. Love's sweet, buttery, perfect pastries.

"Thank goodness."

He swallowed and looked at me. "You know she'll be back, right?"

"Really? Even though I broke her plate?"

"You'd have to do a lot more than that to stop Ms. Love," he said.

I'm currently working on a plan.

Lunchtime Recollection

Joseph Byrd

Suddenly, I am
back there, backed in and under where I
once tongued *Don't come in here* against the
Naugahyde, my octopus eyes peeking from the shoal of our couch at
Grandpa Bill's manatee torso, supine on the
living room floor, he who was safety in wake and surge. There is
no fake ink in you, he said without words. Using him for a
table, our toasted cheese sandwiches on his
tummy, we pressed his nipples as doorbells. We let our
Tang-filled Tupperware cups rise and fall on the
wind of his laughter, he who knew how kids could
burn like long-left bread in a pan if they'd been
buttered religiously. He did
not go to school on Sunday. He did not let his
hands do anything other than help us keep paddling through the
sole, sustaining memory of this
foundering family, shipwrecked against itself.

Bible Camp

Myles Weber

The year we met at Camp Lacroix
we stayed out late to watch the moon
eclipsed by our more massive sphere
and made a date for tennis just
two hours hence. (We lived far north
and it was June. The dawn came fast.)

His name, John Luther Christianson,
surpassed my own in verbiage
and piety. His hair was long,
his biceps prominent. He served
half-speed to give his friends a chance.
He read the Russian novels I
knew only several titles of.
Some judged him too intelligent.

Bible Camp

The brain commenced its tricks. It swore
John Luther meant no more to me
than I to him. As a friend, both fast
and best, I sought to form a bond
of rare intensity without
corporeal entanglements—
a lie I made myself believe.

The night we watched the moon shade rust,
a smile of wonderment was his
response to nature, not to me.
These decades hence just such boys,
now men, would make most perfect
candidates for proper friends. Their smarts,
their gentleness toward sons and wives,
the comfort they effect in their
own skin compose a potent mix
in middle age. I vow to keep
my distance, keep my feelings and
my hands in check. In junior high
I vowed the same. And temperaments
like mine, with age and wisdom gained,
will fool themselves as easily.

In the Bargain Basement

Naomi Azriel

Chop your vegetables with great care
you never know what comes next

your leg muscles cramp from the long journey
through one city block after another

in search of milk   of diapers   of a sign
the war is coming to an end

I lied   there are no vegetables   no diapers   no milk
there is only war   city blocks   leg cramps

which you caress in this damp
basement between loud explosions

how to feed the baby?

In the Bargain Basement

ten of your neighbors gather
in an attic to recite *the mourner's kaddish*

almost imperceptible, someone is playing the piano

I am here   I am here now

Christian

Birgit Lennertz Sarrimanolis

In the winter of 1943, I was eight, a youngster full of life in the years the war crushed the life out of many people. My family lived in Aachen, close to the border to Holland, and the fighting, at times, seemed near. Years later I understood that my recollections were based more on gruesome images we boys conjure in our imaginings than on what we actually saw.

In reality we did not encounter soldiers hanging, bloodied and limp, on barbed-wire fences. We did not see much of the artillery fire that lit up the purple sky when British fighter planes droned overhead. We lived through the days giving little thought to the food shortage or women without husbands or the coal that never sufficed to heat the *Kachelofen* in the corner. We sat and listened to the radio in the evening, not because we felt the impact of armored divisions rumbling through the German streets or the B-17 bombers dominating the skies but because it had become a routine. Even on the nights we ran to the *Luftschutzkeller* amid wailing sirens and feet echoing on the cobblestones, we cowered among others with more excitement than apprehension glistening in our eyes. The next morning, after the danger passed, we stumbled home, weary and unkempt, and found that our apartment block still looked the same, almost disappointingly so. Still, those years left an indelible imprint on us. For me it was not so much the war that did so. It was a boy I met.

Leaden clouds hung overhead when I ran from the flat on the Melatener Strasse. Mother's shrill admonishments resounded down the stairwell, but I pretended not to hear. It was a Saturday, I remember, because I did not have to be in school and had, instead, spent much of the morning in the butcher shop line, food ration coupons in hand. We were one of the lucky families, Mother always said, because there were so many of us. Six children. The two youngest were still drinking mostly milk, so their ration coupons for meat and bread could be divided among the rest of us.

"Ask Kurt for the bones," Mother said. "I'll make *Gemüsesuppe* tonight."

The prospect of eating cabbage soup again, as well as the long wait in the cold, sullied my mood. I stood, one of many in a long queue with red, swollen hands clasping stringy net bags. When it was finally my turn, Kurt wrapped the bones in newspaper. His apron was smeared red and stretched taut over his stocky frame. His small, watery eyes were surrounded by wrinkles in his wide face. He gave me a breathy smile and inquired after my mother.

"Tell her I will call on her soon," he said as I turned to go. I did not respond. I did not know what to say. It had been too long since I remembered my father.

When I returned to the flat, I tried to step quietly onto the creaking floorboards. I listened for a moment and heard the splashing of my youngest siblings in the large, wooden bathtub. Mother was heating water on the stovetop for their weekly bath, and I could hear scrubbing sounds and squeals from the bathroom. I tiptoed into the kitchen and carefully placed Kurt's wrapped package on the kitchen table. I retreated toward the open door again.

Temporarily freed from chores, I set out in search of Joachim and Ernst. It was our habit to carouse the neighborhood, looking for various forms of entertainment. We jumped onto the steps of a passing street trolley, clinging onto the metal bars until the conductor's infuriated "*Raus!*" sent us scampering onto the cobblestones below. Near the *Staufenplatz* we clambered among the ruins and explored recesses that the bombing had not destroyed. The houses stood gaping. The sun glittered on glass shards that jutted from window frames.

Ernst scurried up the diagonal spine of a crumbling wall. The bricks provided natural, albeit precarious, steps for him, and his shoes scuffled up a cloud of sand and grit. He hollered to us from the top, imitating the nasal monotony of Frau Kruse, our schoolteacher. Joachim encouraged him with shouts and laughter. I wandered on myself between the blackened walls to an area that must have served, once upon a time, as an *Innenhof*, a central courtyard between buildings. We had one for our block as well, a central area that provided the pulse of life, where neighbors passed, nodding at each other, remarking about the weather. Windows looked down upon it, and in summer months housewives called to each other from behind geraniums on the sill. Now the flagstones lay cracked and unaligned. Weeds pushed up from underneath. A perambulator with a missing wheel stood under a tree. An abandoned clothesline hung loosely between its wooden posts.

I walked and the ground suddenly gave way beneath my feet. I fell, shrieking, into the blackness below. I landed abruptly and felt a sharp pain shooting up my leg. Nausea overcame me. Dim light penetrated the shaft I had fallen through. I could barely discern my surroundings. My plummet had been swift and ruthless. Swallowing the bitter taste that rose in the back of my throat, I squinted into the darkness. I gave out another startled cry.

Christian

A boy, maybe a few years older than myself, crouched in the darkness, looking wide-eyed at my unexpected intrusion. His face was smeared with soot. The flicker of a candle stub beside him cast eerie shadows onto his features. He jerked up suddenly and I scrambled backward, throat constricted in horror. A shooting stab radiated up my leg.

"Be still," the boy growled and squatted down beside me. I did not dare speak. He touched my ankle and edged off my shoe. He wore trousers that were ripped at the knee and a woolen pullover that was either gray or dirty, I couldn't tell which. The marks on his face, I made out, were from grease, not soot. They also blackened his fingers. His lips were pressed into a firm line as he concentrated on my foot, poking here and there and glancing at me with black eyes to register my reaction.

"It's not broken," he finally decided. He placed his hands on his thighs and straightened himself. In a corner he rummaged through a wooden box and produced a kitchen cloth, which he began ripping into strips.

"I'll bandage it," he announced.

He was quite deft with his hands, I saw as he wrapped my foot tightly. When he finished he sat back on his heels and regarded his work with satisfaction.

"I'm going to work with the doctors when I join the war," he told me. An almost wistful expression overcame his features. "I can't wait to turn fifteen."

I stared at him.

An annoyed look crept over his face.

"Have you lost your tongue?" he demanded.

My voice came as a croak. "How?"

"First I'll go to the *Flak*," he said.

In those days boys as young as fifteen were ordered to operate the anti-aircraft artillery to defend against the allied air raids. By that winter the war situation had turned upon itself. On the radio we heard that Stalingrad had fallen, and German soldiers unable to retreat had either died or were in captivity. It was not long before all remaining soldiers still left in Aachen were ordered to the Russian front. Young boys were pulled out of school to take their places at the *Flak* and taught to shoot airplanes from the skies.

In the cellar a lit candle let shadows dance along the cinder wall. A shelf ran along it, on which I made out several objects, neatly lined up. I pulled myself up with an effort and hobbled over to it. An alarm clock, round and shiny with a white face and a large winding key, stood in the middle. Several books with worn covers leaned against each other. A couple of bicycle lamps were positioned carefully. The smoothness of an old mahogany music box caught my eye. I reached for it.

"Don't!" the boy snapped. "You'll break it!"

He took the box from the shelf and ran his fingers over its lid. More softly he said, "It's precious, you know."

I gazed at him with respect.

"What do you do with them?" I inquired, gaining courage.

"I fix them." He carefully placed the music box among his treasures on the shelf. "Sometimes I sell them."

The silence lengthened.

"When *I'm* old enough I'm going to join Papa," I declared. It was our aspiration, Ernst's and Joachim's and mine, to contribute to the war effort, to be regarded as our fathers and older brothers on the front were.

The boy wiped grease off a screwdriver with a rag. He placed it into the wooden box.

"Papa's in Austria. At least Mother thinks so," I continued. "Where's yours?"

"Dead," the boy said flatly.

"Oh… Did he die on the front?" I asked after a moment.

"No, at home," he told me. "Rheumatic fever."

I fell silent and tried to imagine what it would be like not to have Papa. It wasn't difficult because I did not see him very often anyhow. He had been away for so long. The morning he left we all stood on the platform at the railway station. Before he climbed onto the train, Papa said to Mother, "Be hopeful that the war is turning now. But I fear we will still see the enlistment of Dieter and Josef." He was referring to my two older brothers, but then he looked sadly down at me and said, "Pray they will not pull in Bernd as well."

The train chugged out of the station with a piercing whistle. I ran alongside, trying to catch up with the locomotive before the platform ended. At bedtime Mother held me tightly. I stood patiently, knowing that her embrace wouldn't last forever.

I heard Ernst and Joachim's calls, distant and muffled, calling for me. The boy looked up warily, as though afraid his refuge would be discovered. I limped over to the ladder propped against the wall and climbed up, one step at a time, dragging my hurt ankle. I gave him the semblance of a smile. He watched me sullenly. Then I hauled myself into the gray day again.

That evening Mother hollered and fussed simultaneously. She bathed my foot in a dish of warm water, throwing away the makeshift bandage. My ankle had swollen up, and the bruised area had taken on an array of purples and blues. Mother's hands were gentle but her voice was strained. She demanded an explanation. I fell into a cellar, I told her. A boy I had come upon perchance had bandaged my foot. Nothing more.

Mother kept me indoors the following day. I limped irritably about the small flat, snapping at my younger sisters and brother as they pushed toy trains across the wooden floor. I sat down at the kitchen table, irritated. Nothing kept my attention. Mother sat at her sewing machine in her bedroom. Herr Schultz at the tailor shop had long ago recognized her dexterity with the needle as well as the shortcomings of her purse. He often sent mending that she could finish at home while still caring for her young children.

When Mother went out briefly to get milk at the dairy, I sifted through the bottom drawer of the dresser. Papa's shirts lay neatly pressed. The watch he wore to nice occasions was in the long cardboard box he bought it in. His socks were rolled into tight balls, and his ties were folded in a small stack. I, however, couldn't remember him wearing anything but his uniform.

I looked out of the window. Down on the Melatener Strasse the day progressed. Frau Petersen, handkerchief tied over her hair, rumbled a handcart with her allotted share of firewood from the lumberyard. Across the street Herr Jensen was talking to Frau Brugge across a fence. Frau Brugge's laundry flapped stiffly in the crisp air.

When Dieter and Josef had leave from their posts at the *Flak*, I helped by laying the plates. Mother glanced curiously at me from time to time but kept her attention on the comments my older brothers made about what their superiors said about the war. I avoided my mother's eyes. I ladled soup and cut bread and even said grace before eating.

On Monday morning Mother inspected my ankle and decided I was well enough to attend school. I could not believe my luck. Brightening, I lurched into an upright position. Once outside I ran, buckling, toward the school.

The day at school crawled. Twice Frau Kruse caught me staring out the window. To my annoyance, she told me it was my turn to clean the blackboard, empty the water bucket, and straighten the chairs for the following morning. Joachim and Ernst waited outside, shuffling from one foot to another in the cold, but I ran, heedless of their cries, in the direction of the *Innenhof*.

The cellar was empty. I sat on an apple box and waited. At last the boy climbed down the ladder, a bulging burlap sack slung across his shoulder. He jumped when he saw me and scowled. "What are you doing here?"

"Waiting for you," I replied.

"I don't like it when people come snooping around my place," he muttered and started emptying the contents of his sack. "Shouldn't you be at school?"

"School's over," I told him. It never occurred to me to ask him the same.

From the sack the boy produced a few screws, which he placed into the wooden box. The head of a hammer, some tinfoil, two cans of herring fish, the end of a loaf of bread. He pulled open the lid of one of the cans with a metallic click and pierced a piece of herring onto a knife. He ate while surveying his new acquisitions with dark eyes. I watched silently. He looked up and offered me some bread. A coldness filled the hollow of my stomach. I shook my head.

The boy set out again after eating. I trailed behind, in a cold drizzle, and watched as he kept his eyes on the rubble. Every now and again he stopped, picked something up from the debris, cast it aside again. Sometimes he pocketed it. He did not speak to me. A long while passed and my ankle started to throb. Suddenly he turned and held out his palm. On it lay some screws.

"The small ones are always useful," he explained. I tried to look attentive. "I often find things on which you can use them. But the bigger ones are good for radios. If you find either, you must keep them."

Thus our shaky friendship began, propelled only by the common purpose of uncovering the means of his meager livelihood. His enterprise of repairing and selling objects fascinated me. I spent the next three days walking about with my head stooped low, eyes constantly searching. The screws I found were usually of no use to him. Still, he was willing to place them into his wooden box. I watched him repair the items we rescued from the rubble. I tried to assist in companionable silence, handing him tools, shifting myself out of the light that came through the cellar shaft. One Saturday afternoon I accompanied him to the flea market behind the church, where he set up a crate to display his accumulated treasures. On rare occasion a passerby took pity and tossed him a few coins.

I slipped out of school whenever Frau Kruse's attention was directed elsewhere. Joachim and Ernst, befuddled but loyal, invented excuses for me. I kept the boy and his cellar my secret. I feared he would dematerialize if I spoke too loudly.

One day my brothers Dieter and Josef received papers ordering them to their positions on the front. They had been with the *Flak* for the past year, where they worked the anti-aircraft fire and slept in a bunkhouse. The compound was only a bus ride from our house but visitors were discouraged. Mother sometimes paid the fare to walk by the high, barb-wired fence, hoping she would catch a glimpse of her two boys. Mother packed Dieter's and Josef's rucksacks with the belongings they were allowed to take to the war. The little ones stared with large eyes when Dieter and Josef put on crisp uniforms and slung their packs over their shoulders, pride shining in their faces. It was time, once again, to go to the railway station.

After their departure I spent less and less time at home. I sought out the boy in his cellar whenever I could. I walked with him for hours until blisters formed on my feet. I sneaked apples and potatoes from Mother's pantry to bring to him. I brought him the extra woolen blanket from my bed.

I returned to the flat only when dusk cloaked the town. After the little ones were in bed, Mama sat at the kitchen table with Kurt, their fingers wrapped around enamel mugs of tea. Mother lowered her eyes when I entered the room, and Kurt laughed a little too loudly. I answered their questions in monosyllables and slipped behind my curtained partition. Later, after Mother had mumbled to Kurt under her breath and the door fell shut with a quiet click, I peered from behind the curtain. A watery smile softened Mother's mouth for an instant. Then she straightened, tucked a loose strand of hair into her tight bun, and took the cups over to the sink.

It wasn't long before Frau Kruse, the schoolteacher, came to our flat. She inquired about my absences at school and my inattention to homework. Mother's cheeks flushed as she handed Frau Kruse a cup of tea. They discussed me for some time and then spoke about the Russian front, exchanging information they gleaned from sources other than the radio. Frau Kruse patted Mother's forearm as she got up to leave, and Mother pressed her thin lips together.

Mother was angry but her fury was silent and hopeless. She kept me by her side. Her eyes wore a dangerous gleam whenever my gaze strayed toward the front door. Her anger was channeled through me, not at me. I tried not to provoke her.

The days grew colder and an icy wind swept between the buildings. Mother kept the stove fire going even after we went to bed. In the evenings Kurt came and sat with us at the kitchen table while we listened to the radio. His red face wore a doleful expression, and I decided that his look was not cast on simply for my mother's benefit.

In the middle of the night, Mother shook me out of a heavy slumber. The sirens were wailing as they hadn't in many nights.

"*Schnell, schnell.*" Mother hurried me and my younger siblings quickly down the stairwell. Outside people were running frantically, calling to each other above the sound of the sirens. We scrambled to the *Luftschutzkeller* and were pushed down the stairs by people behind us. The heavy trapdoor was shut with a bang just as the bombs fell thundering above us, shaking the earth. I huddled close and looked to Mother and the baby clinging to her neck. I could find no comfort in her blank stare. People sat with their eyes fixed above each other's heads, shoulders pulled in tightly. Children whimpered and cried as the walls trembled. Some women began to sing a song to the children, their eyelids pressed shut. I wished they would stop.

I closed my eyes and thought about the last afternoon I had spent in the cellar. The boy had managed to repair a radio, and when it picked up a shortwave, we whooped exaggeratedly at his success. A war song was playing, something about the march of our feet keeping time to the rhythm of our years. The tempo was quick and percussive. I got to my feet and performed a jilted dance. Both of us laughed so hard that tears streamed down our cheeks.

A calmness befell me then, and when I opened my eyes, the shelter did not seem quite so claustrophobic anymore. The ache behind my eyes had dulled. When the sirens stopped in the early morning, I disregarded Mother's cries and ran all the way to the *Staufenplatz*. I rounded the corner to the courtyard and saw that it gaped as a huge hole. The cellar had vanished. Stunned, I sat down on a pile of bricks. It occurred to me then that I had never asked him his name. Nor had he ever known mine.

Still Life with Gray Suitcase

—after a photograph by Diego Herrera Carcedo
Irpin, Ukraine March 6, 2022

Judith H. Montgomery

The gray suitcase waits alone on the blown street.
Its plastic skin pocks with shot. Its zipper gleams.
The little wheels await direction. The suitcase sits,
patient as a dog at its master's grave. It is not a dog.
It is a locked box. Crammed within—perhaps a hasty
nest of shirts. A comb. A sleeve of snatched family
photographs. And the one who packed it—wrecked,
body flung like litter to the curb. The hand that held
the handle bleeds the street. The rest, hidden beneath
a faded cloth flapped open to settle—no, to cover—
the sight. Someone knelt here, by the body, by
the stopped suitcase, its abandoned map. Then fled.

Klee

Matthew J. Spireng

It wasn't expensive—$25
at the flea market, but she
passed up the abstract painting

on silk because her walls
were near full and an African mask
distracted her. When she came through

again and saw the painting
no longer offered, she asked
the vendor about his sale. None,

he told her, explaining a friend
had seen the painting and examined it
with a magnifying glass. He found

a signature: Klee, Paul Klee,
and the vendor removed it
from his offerings. The $25 painting

she'd passed up was worth at least
five figures, she learned after
returning home. But she had

the African mask, and with
a little rearranging found
the room to hang it.

Moss: Facts and Fictions

Merridawn Duckler

Travels by wind, a hitch hiker like my thoughts on the drive
to the ocean, a rider all my life. Not particular, that spore,
feeling the way forward, and yet very particular in that
conditions must be right, for moss to land,
for me to talk to anyone, sitting alone at breakfast
in the over-floral-y sit room at Nye Beach,
battered with storms, no moss clings on that.

Moss and me like divided, fragmented, shaken
landscapes, even as I pour the slurry yogurt
some misguided souls believe will help growth.
It will not. Moss wants a place at the table,
lightly trod upon. Also: I want some contact,
but not too much; natural and barefoot,
not the stomp, or shuffle. Moss and me both bounce
back, though not well from well-dressed,
depressed couple drowned in raisin bran.

No one is allergic to me, I say, I am not a parasite, I say
under my breath, eating in small bites, and also: stay,
damned non-parasite, stay and engage. You are not
mold, in fact mold and you are rarely found in the same room.

Then someone does sit, his kind, scruffy face clean
his silver earring earned, his eyes not sad but measured,
no ring. A true moss versus lichen and algae
(nothing against them) (as I have nothing against the waves that eat
     the sand)
lands light in receptive landscape, a solo traveler.

His children arrive, beautiful souls he can't
quite believe he made from division.
Not that we would ever discuss, since we are strangers,
at breakfast. OK, I can thrive on a surface, but can't be too
superficial as I speak toward and away and hope I mirror
the waves, in my grey-blue eyes, his grey- brown, damp.
Should he want me to hold back tears, well, I will
also spit and piss and sweat,
sticky on the banks, moss and me can hold dirt.

And listen this idea that I contain disreputable insects
is unearned. I am bigger than that, though I am a short
statured thing, even a medium sized wave can knock me
down without needing the ladder of a metaphor. But, hey,
we are talking. It is going. I sit in my chair, fairly calm
rolling inside, back and forth, a moss, an airborne expression.
Parting is hard to figure
out: if I leave too soon, the patch withers. I stay too long,
The patch dies. I can't be responsible for everything
I am responsible for. Out our now collective view
the ocean is the color of old plate, and in the cracks of things
terms take root. That is all. Try and remember the color

I tell myself as we pleasantly say goodbye. I like how
they make me stand a moment. Now my part is still here.
Now I am the color of something we made pass over us
then come home, for one moment.
Then return to spreading ordinary breath,
that lies everywhere
and lives in everything.

The Bottom of the Pool

Emily Eddins

I have watched the light
In my bright shining boy dim
A permanent shadow across your face
I hear it now
A swarm of bees
In your brain
The buzz unbearable
A penny for your thoughts
All I own for
Your thoughts to change
Are you sleeping in
Or are you dead?
And then a thud upstairs
Did you just kick the chair
Out from under you?
I have now proven
A mother can hold
Her breath for months
Every morning I wait
For the text bubbles
To float up like air from
The bottom of the pool

Then I'll know
Your heart is still beating
So mine can too

First

Heather Bartos

The guy using the washer next to ours is wearing a pair of red pajama pants decorated with chickens, bottles of hot sauce, and the words "keepin' it spicy."

Hey, I'm not going to judge. When it gets to be laundry day, strange things happen. And twenty years ago, I might have taken the time to strike up a conversation with him, trying not to inhale his cologne that smells like bug spray.

Now? I just don't want him anywhere near Veronica. She is sitting on one of the hard plastic chairs with a view of the dryer, pencil out, glasses on, squinting at some math I wouldn't be able to do even if someone held me at gunpoint. Because, God forbid, if she didn't stare at her math, she might have to make conversation.

I try to get her attention. "Hey. If you want, we could get donuts and coffee?"

She shrugs. "That's okay."

She's not going to make this easy.

She used to like to go to the store with me. We would wander in the bakery aisle, searching for the sweetness, the colored frosting molded into flowers and rainbows. We would look at the bouquets and pick the one we were going to buy if we had enough money after groceries. I taught her the names of the flowers, how the name "Veronica" was also a flower name but lots of people wouldn't know that.

But she knew, because I taught her.

Mr. Spicy gives Veronica a glance. He takes in her pink high-top Converse shoes, her faded jeans, her long gray hoodie that says "UC San Francisco" pulled over her dark hair. She's better at braiding it than I ever was. It used to slip through my fingers like silk, escaping any shape I tried to force.

How could I have even thought about leaving her to get donuts and coffee with Mr. Spicy sniffing around?

"We could get lunch when we are done," I offer.

"I have work to do," she says.

The cause of this cold front is on the kitchen table in our apartment. It's an application for federal student aid. She asked me to tell her how much I made.

"Enough," I said. "Enough to take care of you."

"But not enough," she said, "to pay for college."

It's this counselor at the school, filling her head with all of this college talk, how she has to go, how she won't *be* anyone if she doesn't go, how she will be the first one in our family to go, and won't that be *something*.

Back when she was little, there was lots of talk every year that sounded like this. Santa was going to give her everything she wanted. Santa even asked her to write a list.

Extra shifts at the care home, long hours with a babysitter who took most of the pay, was Santa. Santa wiped urine off the floor so he could buy colored plastic, bikes with training wheels and ribbons on the hand grips, dolls with platinum hair, canisters of colored Play-Doh, all the shine and brightness that never comes for free.

Now Santa is asking for information. How much am I worth? How much am I willing to pay?

Are parents ever done paying?

"Oops," says Mr. Spicy, bumping into Veronica. I give him a look that says, *Yeah, sure*, and sit in the seat between them.

"So, you go to UC?" he asks.

"No," she says. "Maybe later."

"Education is important," he says. "Good for you."

"Yeah, well," she says, with a little laugh, "my mother doesn't think so."

"Veronica," I say. "You know that's not true."

I want to ask who taught her how to count her allowance. I want to ask who else taught her that it was never enough, that it didn't count.

"My mom," she tells this stranger, "doesn't want to help me to go to college. All she has to do is fill in some paperwork, but she won't do it."

My eyes blur as I watch the laundry spinning, all of our intimate things on display. People with cash don't have to put on a show for the neighbors.

"All of the other kids sent it in already," Veronica says.

"If you get a loan, you can pay it off," says Mr. Spicy.

"I know," says Veronica. "My counselor says where there's a will, there's a way."

There's no will, I want to tell her. No Santa Claus left you a million bucks so you can go to a UC, so that you can be first.

You have *always* been first, Veronica. You just can't see that. Even though I gave you glasses, you still can't see.

"Well, good luck," says Mr. Spicy. "See you around."

Veronica smiles. "See you."

I think about our last fight. She had left the door unlocked all night.

"You can't do that," I told her. "I don't feel safe."

"Nobody's going to take anything," she argued. "Who would want it?"

Our door can't be open, welcoming whatever comes, and closed to protect us at the same time.

For just a little longer, we share the same door.

I glance down at her math. Then I look one more time to be sure.

She has my tax return, from the guy at the mall, and that application for student aid. And she's filling it out.

"How were you going to get my signature?" I ask.

She looks up at me. I remember the time I picked you up at daycare, the only time you got in trouble. You pushed another kid during a race, and she fell, and you ran right over her so you could be first. You glared at me, eyes glittering, your delicate chin sharp and pointed as a weapon of war.

The dryer buzzes. I pull out the laundry, straightening before folding, while you get ready to run.

Age of Reason

Jacob Reina

If it is set against my will—rekindling
A life, a marriage, the art of raising
Myself up well enough each day
To raise a human child—if it is—
To cluster together in pleasant photos
And smile for the camera
(As I demand you all to smile)—
To become more than your bracketed title,
More than your conversational afterthought
Or a forgotten iron on your ankle—
If it set against my will—waking
And dreaming, sleeping dreamlessly—

May I allow myself the great honor to lose myself
In the riverside's pathways, overgrown with weeds
(And in this very way, shall I return to you—you
Off losing yourself with graceful but petrified steps
In the noisy crowded street bazaar of my memory)?

Let me find you there as a handful of gold
(Flaked and floating upon the river like dead men)
And forge you by fire to make your value life-saving

(Debt-killing, college-funding, a shortcut, the retiring from life)
And let you find me broken, as a shattered ceramic vase
That is being swept beneath the table of a vendor selling rugs.

This is the honesty in life; this is that cherished thing called Reason
Held so dearly in the floating flame you call The Real World.

You said last night I must tell you where I've gone—
I've gone to river, to unbury my laughter's bones.

Impermanent

Tom Cullerton

Objects continue to exist
when they can't be seen.
Infants learn the skill:
they remember the ball
under a blanket.

The new moon, lit by our star,
with the old moon in her arm.
We learn to trust the uncovering,
the return. A wave pulls back
with a hiss about depth and darkness.

We learn about moon, tides,
about seasons. The solstice
in winter brings back light,
brings a memory of warmth,
green thoughts, from the rain,

Impermanent

from the cover of leaf rot.
We learn to trust what isn't there—
the next day,
dawn is becoming:
we learn to compare.

Until a day begins
with an absence,
and there is only the thought of a friend—
in the quiet applause
of a flight of pigeons.

An infant doesn't know
"too young," there is no separate,
permanent.
The day after a death
is a new day,

the next day—
a hopping crow shuffles
the dark weight of winter
as he pokes and pulls
from the cold earth.

The Day the Queen Died

Paul Brownsey

The day the Queen died was the day we drove together into the city to consult a lawyer about our divorce. We planned to use the Simplified Procedure available under Scots law, which doesn't require lawyers and court, because we were entirely in agreement that our marriage had broken down irretrievably and—perhaps more likely when two men are divorcing than when a man and a woman are—there were no disputes about children, nor about money or anything else. However, the Simplified Procedure requires a minimum of a year's separation and you have to state when you "ceased to live with your spouse." Niven and I had found it convenient and civilised to continue to live under the same roof until I was to move to America and a new life with Madison—in the autumn, probably—so we needed to know whether ceasing "to live with" your spouse ruled out sharing an address or whether it was just a polite way of referring to sex and sharing a bed.

We continued to share meals, which was also civilised. In easy chat over dinner I noticed that there still came, from both of us, the conversational ploys, allusions, standing jokes, tones of voice, that had ridden on the flow of our love but now resembled practices surviving only as quaint folk customs following the death of a civilisation. As we ate dinner after our visit to the lawyer, trays on our knees as usual, Niven's melanzane as tasty as always, the TV news was increasingly ominous about the Queen. Her doctors were "concerned," seemingly a codeword for something very serious indeed being up; her children were heading for Balmoral as quickly as possible; there'd been hurried consultations and exits in the House of Commons involving leading figures. We ate in silence. Then they cut to Huw Edwards, whom we'd already seen in a black suit and tie, as if he'd been previously tipped off, and he announced the Queen's death.

"A day on which the world as you and I know it is passing away," Niven said.

Between repeated announcements of the death, commentators told us we should never see her like again, it was the end of an era, she had held us together, she was a shining example of steadfastness and dedication and duty, she was for the whole nation the ideal grandmother everyone yearned for.

"Easy to say that about someone you don't know," I said. "A blank surface you can project anything on to make them the person who makes up for all the lacks in your life."

"Like when you see someone and fancy them," Niven said.

The phone went—our landline. Niven handed me the phone, saying, in the civilised way we'd developed, "Your fiancé." He went off to the kitchen to do the washing-up.

"Hi, Roger, honey. I had to call you just as soon as I heard of your loss." Unconditional concern flowed through that gentle transatlantic accent and down the line. It came from a high place where feelings were whole and pure. It would have spoiled the moment if I'd said that I felt no loss; though, indeed, Madison's voice seemed to be conjuring a feeling of loss in me, like he knew better than I did what was within me.

Madison Lorimer was a professor at a college near Philadelphia called Swarthmore. The previous spring he'd given the Stevenson public lectures on politics at Glasgow University. He looked like an over-grown student, as though he'd been so busy learning things that age had had no opening to creep up on him, but he radiated authority. At question time I asked whether politics could be a form of religion. The woman chairing the lecture approached me afterwards to say Madison would like to talk more with me about my question. I was nervous when led up to him, but his eyes and smile put me at my ease at once, assuring me that nothing I could say would be beneath his notice. I felt honoured when he suggested, rather solemnly, that we have a drink at his hotel. I texted Niven that I'd be late home, and then Niven sank to the back of my mind or below it.

Madison insisted that what I'd said at the lecture was very in-sightful.

"Oh. Really? I mean, but, see, I dropped out of university."

"A lot of the best people drop out of university. I'm sure you're one of the best." It felt as though he'd shone a light on potential I'd not appreciated in myself during my up-and-down life with Niven.

Yes, we mentioned details of our lives—that I was married to Niven, that Madison was single—but these seemed like routine things you barely think about as you enter them on a form. When we moved from the bar to the foyer, neither of us said Goodnight, nor did we say anything else about how the night was to progress or might progress, but when he set off up the stairs to his room, I went with him, side by side, and though there had been no invitation to do so, he showed no sign of finding this this presumptuous. It was as if I were his equal. My life unconnected to him was neither here nor there, shrivelled away.

Back home the next morning, I told Niven, "I guess we both knew that something like this was bound to happen sooner or later."

"Bound to happen, absolutely. No choice in the matter. And if it was bound to happen, then better sooner than later."

I hurried to make it clear that I hadn't attended the lectures with any such thing in mind. I added, "It tells us a lot about how our feelings, yours and mine, have evolved over time."

"The one you think is 'The One' is never The One." Niven smiled.

The remainder of Madison's stay in Scotland had been something outside of time, cocooned in love so certain that his scheduled departure caused me no distress at all. Later I even fell to wondering whether I could have had some sort of foreknowledge that before leaving the UK he was going to propose marriage and I was going to say yes to a future with him on the beautiful campus of the college near Philadelphia. When I went across in the summer, he welcomed me to America as to his private domain.

"Raised up into a new world. Not at all like a passing crush on a work colleague," Niven said, when I described my visit.

The night they announced the Queen's death, Madison spoke about the effect the Queen had on his mother, who'd been a Democratic member of the House of Representatives when she visited for the 1776 bicentennial celebrations. There'd been a hoo-ha over the band playing *The Lady is a Tramp* while the Queen danced with President Ford. Introduced to the Queen, Madison's mother couldn't restrain an urge to apologise as if she'd been personally responsible. In a confiding voice that acknowledged Mrs. Lorimer to be one of the few people who could see sense about the incident, one whose regular counsel she wished she could avail herself of, the Queen replied, "Someone once told me that the song is ironical—the lady most certainly isn't a tramp—so it's perfectly all right." There was grace in this that Mrs. Lorimer sought for the rest of her life to emulate. "And if she could have that effect on my mother, think of the effect she must have had on so many people in your country, just by being there as a representative of values and qualities that people cherish in their hearts. Her death will affect them, too. Perhaps in ways they don't realise."

I wanted to say the Queen's death would have no effect on me, but Madison made me feel that that wasn't what a nice person would say, so instead I said that the death of a mother-figure to the nation might mean more to Niven, given that his own mother had cut off all contact with him twenty-four years before when he told her he loved me and we were getting a flat together. "If that's how she wants to play it," he'd said, and shrugged. Madison and I could talk about Niven without reticence, our love uniting us in honest consideration for him. I added, "If you know your own mother warts and all—and it's nearly all warts in Vera's case—that could lead you to idealise a national mother-figure," though when I thought about it I could recall no sign of Niven venerating the Queen. Madison could still flummox me into saying such things.

After the call I went to the window and stared out, hands in pockets.

I realised I was doing something absurd, looking to see how the world had been changed by the death of the Queen. In the dusk, the bungalow opposite ours was silently the same, the hills outlined on the horizon against a strip of cool green sky were the same. *Of course* there was no difference. How could there be?

Yet something had happened to the world. Once upon a time, perhaps, people believed the death of a monarch disrupted the movements of the stars in their courses. The death of Elizabeth II hadn't done that, but the world had come unstuck from my experience of it, my plans, my feelings.

In the bungalow opposite ours lived an irritating pair called May and Derek Gifford. Their garden hedge spread out over the pavement, and the Giffords parked their car, not in their drive but three-quarters on the pavement, almost up against the overgrown hedge. Pedestrians—and a neighbour who uses a wheelchair—were forced out into the road by the Giffords' selfishness.

But tonight, something had been sucked out of the atmosphere. The Giffords' capacity to exasperate wasn't there. They were people, that was all; their hedge was just something that grew, as hedges naturally do; their car was just a means of transport. The fact that soon I should see the Giffords and their car and hedge no more had disappeared. On the horizon, the hills were bare products of impersonal forces, stripped by the Queen's death of all memories that I had walked there with Niven, he less enthusiastic in an old pair of my boots that leaked.

It was the same inside the house. Linkages were broken. The divorce papers, laid casually on a side-table when we came back from the lawyer, were inert, disconnected from anyone's plans. The clatter of washing-up from the kitchen was nothing to do with the cosy routine of home. The man with a scourer doing the washing up was neither someone I was leaving nor someone I wasn't leaving.

The phone rang. Again Niven picked up.

"My mother for you." The cool civilised PA keeping emotion out of his voice as he handed me the phone. It was, however, an occasion for emotion—indeed, for astonishment. This was the first time she'd spoken to Niven or me since the great excommunication when we set up home together.

I ought to have said, "Yes?" in a who's-this-bothering-me? drawl, but I said it in a voice clipped by dread. Perhaps I sensed that what was coming on this night when things had lost their linkages.

"Roger, this is Vera. Niven's mother. You've heard the news. The Queen." She didn't wait for me to confirm that I had; obviously, no-one could fail to have heard. "I don't know how the country's going to get by without her. Bringing us together like she did in the pandemic, reassuring us we would meet again. Just being there, reminding us of tried and tested values."

I made that brief noise of two notes rising which hovers between agreeing with the other person and merely acknowledging that they've said something.

"Of course, I had the honour to be presented to her." We knew from Niven's sister, who didn't participate in her mother's excommunication of us, that she'd met the Queen at a garden party at the Palace of Holyroodhouse, invited as a member of the Royal Voluntary Service after she'd been the driving force in setting up a visitors' café at a hospital. "I can't remember what I said, probably babbled something silly. I respected her so much. The look in her eyes, the smile—she made me feel I was someone really special—"

"And she would really like to be friends with you if all her royal duties didn't get in the way," I finished for her. I thought how strange it was that a look and a smile from royalty could make people imagine themselves lifted to a realm above their own lives.

"Yes. I felt so, I don't know what the word is..."

"Elevated?"

"Yes," she said, combatively, as though she'd sensed mockery but wanted to claim the word for accuracy. "Elevated. She raised people up to be the best they could be. Saw the best in people. Look how she came to accept Camilla. She was against her at first, well, who wouldn't be, the trouble she caused?"

Was I sinking or was something inching up around me from below? I thought of the occasion years before when, in the horizon hills visible from our house, I'd stumbled into a bog and for a moment thought the ground was rising up to enclose me.

"She must have been so unhappy as a mother. I can understand that. Not what she expected at all. But then she saw how happy she made her son and she wasn't one to hold a grudge. She let him marry her and said, Yes, she was a worthy person and could be the next queen when... well, it's happened now. It's a lesson to us all. Now she's gone we've got to carry on the values she stood for. Tried and tested values, Roger. Bringing people together. Healing divisions. Service. Consideration for others." Said as though I might not have heard of these things. "So I feel that it's particularly appropriate tonight, when we're all mourning her loss, to say I hope you and Niven will come for Christmas dinner this year."

"I shall be in America, starting a new life without Niven," was what I ought to have said, but I heard myself blurt out, "Thank you." The thought came to me that at least it would do something for Niven and that I must always have known that his dismissive attitude towards the breach—"If that's how she wants to play it"—must have covered a lot of pain.

"Very well." Cautiously, as though granting a request from me. "And I have a favour to ask you, Roger. Will you persuade Niven to come? I haven't raised it with him. I wanted to get you onside first. You probably know what he's like. He can be unyielding."

"No, he's not." I had the right to defend Niven against his mother.

"Let's not disagree, Roger, not when the Queen's just... I'm going to say goodnight now."

Anyway, I thought as I put the phone down, I could still cancel later, when I left for the college near Philadelphia and cut Niven out of my life. I tried to think it defiantly.

In the kitchen, I said, "We're going to your mother's for Christmas dinner."

"You and your fiancé?"

"Don't be so bloody silly. You're using the wrong scourer on that pan. It'll scratch."

"I think we agreed, in our civilised way, that household utensils and implements were to be mine." He finished washing the pan without change of scourer, then passed in front of me to put unused mozzarella into the fridge. He bent to clear a space for it. Both the angle of his body as he did this—the body I was so familiar with—and the intentness, heedless of me, with which he carried out the task were suddenly mysteries that I did not know how to fathom.

Tentatively, trying something out, I hugged Niven from behind, slightly surprised, as always, how far around him my arms went. He continued to restack items in the fridge; suddenly his mother's word, "unyielding," struck me as suiting him and I was delighted. I knew there existed a person for whom hugging Niven was an act of homecoming, but Vera's drab phrase "tried and tested" got in the way and I knew I would become that person only after I had completed a period of mourning that began the day the Queen died.

Green Burial

Diane Averill

My soul sister chose to be buried
under the redwood tree her father planted
inside the family acreage on the day of her birth,
her mother's red placenta nourishing the soil.

They wrapped her in the spider-web strong shawl
she made during her last year
and lowered her into the ground
curled as she had once been in her mother's womb.

Human voices rose that day like bird song
around the eighty-foot tree
weaving in and out of the notes on the handmade harp
her son played.
She was dancing in the music.

Eucatastrophe

Julia Hands

It's the aspen leaves quaking,
a decrepit gold in their final days.
The salmon that fight upstream;
how their ghostly scales flake.
The playa receding each summer
into a desert basin, alkaline-coated
Or, the playa each winter, water rising
from the cracks to drown the sand.
How the caterpillar dissolves,
its fine new shell glinting in spring dew.
The bald stump with one new green sprig.
The praying mantis's final, gentle embrace.
It's you and I, just on the precipice of a first meet,
as you wonder how long I'll make you wait.

Dandelions

Amanda Hawk

I find you at our favorite coffee shop,
hunched a little in your chair
to avoid being watched by strangers.

I hold out a bouquet of dandelions
to draw your attention away from the phantom stares,
to me.

I enjoy your smile, the slight smirk blossoms
as you reach out, and for a moment, you touch with
cautious intimacy and vulnerability.

I understand you and your insecurities.
That is what I love the most about you—
your heedful nature.

In the shadows and light of the coffee shop,
I can see your scars shimmer
while you stare at me fiercely.

Dandelions

You grasp the flowers,
playing lightly with the bright yellow petals.
You tell me they taste like your childhood.

You could almost smell the forest—
taste the grit of the dirt roads upon your tongue.
I can't help but smile at your awkwardness.

I want to pop off the heads of the dandelions
and pile them up like tiny yellow marshmallows
on top of your coffee.

Build you sunlight
from their bright yellow petals,
then weave the stems together

until I build you a ladder that stretches to the moon,
so you could touch its face
and press gentle kisses upon its forehead.

I want to pluck the pain from your heart, your body;
present them to you as a beautiful bouquet
of purple, blue, bruises and tears—

just so you can slam it against the ground,
shattering each blossom, exploding each ache
until it is only pieces, remnants scattered around the room.

Dandelions

You take that moment to remind me
many find dandelions to be weeds,
pests infesting their beautiful lawns.

I grab your hand, shaking my head.
I think they just learned to persevere
before everyone else.

Rabbit Moon

Val Killpack

There's no such thing as a yeti, or even a skunk ape, but it's nice to believe. Sasha never ruled out the impossible. Things are only impossible until they're not. When she saw the enormous creature flash through the headlight beams, she didn't even blink. She tended to see things she believed in—even if they weren't real—whenever she tired herself to the bone. She figured she must be hallucinating from lack of sleep, from driving stress, or from the increasing altitude.

Loretta pushed herself upright in the passenger seat, then slumped back and closed her eyes again with a moan.

A blizzard swept their windshield. The wipers torpedoed back and forth and barely kept up. The headlights did little in the grey sky of mid-afternoon. As Sasha looked forward—the car climbing toward the clouds—she thought the snowflakes might be stars, and her journey was beyond the tangible world, destination unknown.

Sasha and Loretta kept moving upward and onward. They climbed past aspens, into spruce forest, and then bristlecone pine. The trees became smaller the higher they went. The road had been scraped clean some time ago, and any patches of exposed pavement had been covered in white. The tires of the beat-up car bounced around in snowy trenches marking the lane. Sasha thought it might be how poorly drilled wagon wheels wriggled in the ruts of muddy, ancient roads. She felt like she might be in a folktale as they pushed through the storm to their remote mountain vacation. The highway slowly filled with powder to blend with the surrounding landscape, a vast blanket of cotton. Sasha looked up at the peak with a wrinkle as the sun began to set.

Loretta dozed in the passenger seat. The sound of engine and tires fighting through the storm had lulled her into dreams. Sasha sat up tall and arched her back to stretch, threw her shoulders back, and rolled her head to loosen up her neck. They had retreated into silence an hour ago when the radio station faded out, and Sasha felt waves of fatigue descending. They hadn't seen another car in hours, and at this momentum, in the degrading conditions, it's doubtful anyone would dare to be out. Sasha remained determined in getting to their reserved mountain cabin and continued. The wind picked up, and when Sasha cracked the window to have a smoke, icy snow gusted across her face. "Mother fucker motherfuck," she said.

Loretta stirred and looked up at her. "Sasha Bunny."

"Motherfuck," she said again.

Loretta grimaced, then smiled and leaned back in her seat. She shivered and turned her head to briefly to meet Sasha's eyes, just for a moment, before looking down.

The sky cleared as they neared the top of the mountain pass. Sasha figured they must be above the clouds and snow. She found what looked like a pull-off on the shoulder and slowed to a stop in the deep snow. The view west had turned orange and pink. "Loretta, babe, let's put our coats on and watch this magnificent sunset. This is what we came to the mountains for."

Loretta sat up from the passenger seat and pushed the door open without a word. She grabbed her coat and slid her arms into the sleeves. "Sasha, come look. The horizon is a rippling magenta dream."

Sasha and Loretta faced the vast western slope, arm in arm, and soaked in the falling light and deepening colors. A white-and-amber-speckled snowshoe hare hopped past them and down the gentle grade into the forest. They both turned and watched it move through the snow. Loretta began to step after it.

"Sasha, we have to follow it. It's our guide. So cute. Those long ears! Do you think it has a family?"

For the first time in a while, Sasha saw a sparkle in Loretta's eyes. "Okay, why not? Just a little way," said Sasha.

The two forged through knee-deep snow down the incline. They followed the hare's tracks into the cover of forest. The iridescence of sunset faded to dusk. Brisk air lightly singed their lungs. Sprays of snow blew off boughs of trees and filled the air. Sasha felt her head spin as she followed Loretta.

Loretta sprung ahead trying to keep up with the fresh tracks of the snowshoe hare. Sasha lost sight of her as they descended into the forest and down the grade of the mountain. First there were pines, after that spruce, and then a clearing of naked aspens. Their wispy bark shined a bright, speckled glow. The storm had waned—only a bit of flurry spiraled in the breeze. The air danced in wisps. Loretta's footprints led past the spacious, naked aspens.

Snow rolled ahead, outward in all directions, shimmering in places, a plush pillow of possibility. The day came to an end; everything turned crepuscular; moonlight peeked through the clouds. Sasha spun around in a dizzy circle. She saw the white wilderness illuminated. Falling stars of snow danced all around her.

"Loretta!" she yelled. "Loretta. Loretta!"

But all she could hear, even faintly make out, was a gentle hush, a soft breeze in the trees, a whisper and a shush.

Sasha froze, held her breath, listened, and took a mental note of where she stood. The forest spread out wide. Below, on the far side of the meadow, in a spacious aspen grove, a snaking river cut a line through the snow. She traced the river's path with her eyes and saw that she stood in the same river. That the snow had given way to water, below. That the icy feeling in her lungs began at her feet. She slogged forward.

To the left, in the east rose a grand mountain, grey rock protruding through the icy vista, and to the right, in the west, like a dream, Sasha could see the faint twinkle of lights resembling a small town or village far in the distance. She plodded to land from the numbing water and headed toward the illumination, but her movements slowed and slowed. And slowed.

Sasha then curled up and slept, just a doze. She dreamed a long, winding dream in those short minutes, of Loretta beside her in bed, postcoital, teasing her. "You're so furry all over, my little rabbit; I love you my sweet fuzzy bunny!" When she awoke, the moon had climbed even higher above. She looked up, inhaled a deep, revitalizing breath, and shook to wake herself up. She gazed up toward the trees and caught a glimpse of the circular bulb in the sky. Foggy halos radiated from the moon, from the aspens, spruces, and pines, and from the ground below.

Early morning is full moon, thought Sasha. She intuitively knew. *Right now, it is waxing.* Her eyes filled with moonlight, her body surged with an electric tingle, and she bounded through the powdery snow. She lurched, then sprung, jumped, and frolicked ahead. She perked her ears high, listened for Loretta, but heard only night. She reached the river and stopped. Perched on hind legs, she shifted her head to the right, to the left, to the right. She felt warm in her cozy angora and decided to rest a minute, and then, after feeling the chill again, she jumped up and hopped around to get the blood flowing.

She looked back left, then straight ahead, for once, and there on the river she saw a Western Slope river otter splashing around. His webbed paws moved seamlessly as he swam up the current. He would dive in, disappear for a few seconds, then resurface and cast his eyes to each side briefly before paddling on. His long, muscular tail propelled him. He shuddered and splashed before diving in again. *He must be looking for fish*, thought Sasha.

She tried not to move. She had heard tales of river otters possessing humans, luring them into their homes, then eating them for dinner. Sasha flattened her ears and buttoned her mouth around her teeth. Her hair stood on end. She focused inward and breathed as deeply as possible. Her vision softened—a gentle gaze. The treacherous notion what this otter could do encircled her, and then she saw it flip from the water directly before her. She stared directly at the river otter and saw it grow and transform. It shape-shifted into a mountaineer, just for a moment, then a beautiful woman, then a child wearing checkered clothing. Sasha began to shiver and wanted to move around to warm up but didn't dare. She saw a severed human head, caught in a net, floating in the river. She blinked and looked again. There stood the river otter.

Sasha looked for Loretta, scanning in every direction, before settling in to watch this rare river otter. She stood behind a spruce tree and peeked around the bark.

The wily otter, after multiple attempts at diving for fish, crawled out of the river, onto the snow-covered bank, and collapsed. After a few minutes of taking rest, he began to scuttle along the bank, just out of range of the water. He sniffed the ground as he inched along. A spot of moonlight lit a patch of snow, and this mesmerizing otter stopped and sniffed. He dug his nose into the snow, wriggled his whole body, snorted, needled into the earth, and with a slap of his tail, he yanked out a large fish, tossed it aside, and dove back into the cavern. He pulled out another, tossed it beside the first, and with a wheeze and a whistle he repeated this until he had a row of seven reddish fish laid out on the bank. He tried to hop, and then he turned and knocked a couple logs toward the water. He pushed them together, one end in the river, the other end atop the bank. From above, he hurdled himself onto this little slide, flat on his belly, and shot rapidly into the creek with a splash. He flapped around, water flying, and crawled back up to slide six more times. Then he grabbed all seven fish and Sasha heard him yell, "###!" The shout rose like the bellow of high wind. *It is a victory shout*, thought Sasha, *undecipherable*.

These fish must have been stored there, perhaps by a local fisherman, and this otter--whom Sasha decided to call Hesperus, which she thought could fit a starlit creature such as this--absconded with his bounty, carrying the seven red fish to his den, which Sasha saw the sullen mouth of, just up the mountain to the east.

Loretta was nowhere to be found. Sasha remembered first seeing Loretta. It was a holiday, a lonely Christmas, and Sasha had worked all day as a coffee barista in a small mountain resort town. The place was filled with flatlanders looking for something open, and they were one of the few. After she closed the shop in the late afternoon, she spent a little time walking in the snow and made her way to a restaurant that was open where she sat at the bar in the back. She wore a men's button-up with a skinny tie. She just happened to sit next to Loretta, and they hit it off. They traded numbers, but it took a while before they began dating. It was that long month of waiting that felt like a journey, as if Sasha was looking for someone she had lost and then found and then lost. In the end they did find each other, which seemed inevitable later. She wasn't sure why she had worried so much that first month, because what could keep them apart, really, she thought. Sasha thought of all this as she perched in the forest like a lost rabbit.

She continued forward in the snow. She crawled, slow-scurried, steadily, and methodically, one foot, another foot, another foot. She stood on the riverbank and peered left, peeked right, and just out of the corner of her eye she saw something jump across the river. It looked like a coyote, but so fast—bigger than a red fox, sleeker than a wild dog—it couldn't be anything else—it had to be a northwestern wolf. A gray wolf reflecting the twilight. Vespertine, most alive in the boundary of day into night. When it leaped the river, golden lightning shot one direction from its mouth and the other from its tail, pure energy drawn from the universe and exploding into the forest. Sasha shuddered.

Sasha followed the gray wolf from the point where it disappeared. Maybe it would lead her to Loretta. Sasha hopped through the brush, a tangle of branches, and peered into an open meadow. A few bunches of mountain brome grass poked above the snow. She gently jumped out of the bush and nibbled on a couple shoots of the barely green strands. She felt something ghostly brush past her but saw nothing. Hair all over her body stood on end. She glimpsed a shadow off into the meadow and focused her little, beady eyes with all her effort.

There before her saw an empty hut, complete with a circular platform and a circular cushion. The platform appeared to slowly spin clockwise, and the small hut was cut so that a horizontal space about the height of a human head was open all the way around, thus allowing anyone seated on the cushion to rotate and have a complete view of the entire field of mountain brome. Sasha jumped around the hut and came upon a fire pit with a grill, much of the snow cleared away. On a skewer laid a roasted lizard. She looked closely and decided it must be a common collared lizard, full grown in size. Next to this delicacy sat a juicy, sliced-open cantaloupe. *Rocky ford cantaloupe and common collared lizard is quite a meal*, thought Sasha. The northwestern wolf looked around, ignoring her—Sasha being so little and harmless. The wolf made a chilling howl, almost a lynx's siren-like scream, but more spectral, lower in tone, a wail from the other side, both sinister and self-mocking. It projected this sound three times. Sasha realized it must be asking: "Is it okay if I take this food? Is this an offering that I may take advantage of? If I should leave it here, will you please reply?" And with that it stood on its hind legs, perked its ears high, and held its head to the wind. It then scooped up the roasted lizard and the cantaloupe halves and walked calmly into the forest and up the grand mountainside to its den.

Sasha rested down into the snow, but before she could decide which way to go on her journey to find Loretta, a Virginia opossum whizzed by juggling seven acorns high into the air. She shook her head to try to wake up the senses. She stomped her feet to move some blood. She looked up to the bright moon in the clear sky to find her reflection. She looked back and the opossum had vanished.

Sasha burrowed deep into the snow drifts. The wind above howled and whistled. The tunnel was cozy, warmer than above, but darker than night. She could barely breathe. She thought she might suffocate. She slowed from panic to the pace of haze. She thought to herself: *control the mind, control the breath; stand on all fours; feel the gravity; see the inside; be one with the hollow.* She excavated the snow, mined her way in.

Sasha wandered in her tunnels. The cold no longer affected her. She looped back into a snow channel she had already forged and followed it around again. And then again. And again. Maybe if she went fast enough, she could catch her own tail. She hopped as fast as she could—and as well as could be expected in a small tunnel—faster and faster. After several laps, she stumbled, dizzy, and fell to her stomach, legs all akimbo. She wanted to fall into dreamland again, but Loretta called to her from her veins. She heard a pulsing in her ears. She tensed up and made small fists.

"Loretta!" she yelled.

"Loretta," she said again.

"Loretta," she said softly.

"Loretta," she said under her breath.

"Loretta."

Sasha dug her way to the surface and walked through the snow. All her senses woke. The river otter's den was just up the mountainside. *Why not?* she thought. *What the hell?* And up the hill she climbed.

"Hello otter," she said. "Hello otter, I'm tired and very hungry and looking for Loretta. She is my heart. Can you help me?"

Otter remained far back in his den, listening to Sasha's hoarse voice, before carefully advancing just beyond the shadow so that he would be visible. He looked over to his stash, then tentatively, with a measured voice and a firm stance, he offered her what he had.

"Yes, my fine young rabbit, I can offer you seven red fish. I found these fish by the river, and I looked, listened, and spoke for their owner three times, but no-one claimed them, so I brought them back to this cozy den. I will offer them to you so that you may find your heart."

Sasha bowed to this auspicious otter and said, "Thank you, otter. Thank you very much. I may come back later to take you up on your generous offer," she said. And with that she ambled on.

Sasha wandered further into the snow. She begged for Loretta like a lost lover the way a mendicant might beg for alms. She aimed her path toward where she had seen the gray northwestern wolf strut off to.

Sasha jumped around to warm up; she spun in a circle, hopped up and down, gyrated to an invisible hula hoop, then scurried off into the night.

She found its den nearby, just a few jumps laterally. Her determination had risen, and she spoke louder this time.

"Hello northwestern wolf," she said with a strong, clear voice. "Gray wolf! Come out gray wolf I need your help. Northwestern wolf, it's an emergency."

"Well in that case," he said from deep within the cavern, "I will offer you my kindly assistance." He continued to speak from the darkness. "In what circumstances have you found yourself that you seek the wisdom of a humble wolf? Where is your spirit, gentle creature, where is your mind?"

"Gray wolf, I have lost my heart. Oh, Loretta! Loretta!" she said. "Where is my heart, gray wolf? I cannot feel my blood anymore. I am a shell, so cold."

"My dearest one, I can give you nourishment, I can warm up your delicate body and bring you back to life. Let me offer you what I acquired on this fine day. I have a wonderful delicacy, a fire-roasted lizard accompanied by rocky ford cantaloupe. These come directly from the earth, from the field watcher's hut. I looked for this field watcher, listened, and called out to their spirit. I believe they have abandoned the post. I believe this field watcher has two journeys inside themself and has pilgrimaged deep into the wood to seek union. Please, my forlorn friend, will you take this meal so that you may have proper energy to find your heart?"

Sasha bowed to this virtuous wolf and said, "Thank you, gray wolf, I may come back later to receive your generous offer." And with that she trundled forward.

Sasha's shoulders fell. She sledged through the wet snow. With an exasperated exhale she collapsed under a tall pine tree. Just when she had begun to settle into a slumber, she heard a loud hissing sound from above.

Click and click-click-click. Then a burst of sneezes.

She gazed upward. A Virginia opossum hung from a high branch.

"Oh, opossum, oh no. Oh no, oh snap. All my toast is now burnt, I'm lost in the garden, my mind is swimming in the water. Get away crazy possum. My mind is banging on the door. My noodle has flipped its lid. A possum is in my mind. Get out, opossum, get thee hence, leave me, leave off, let go of me, let go, let go."

All this vocalization came out as hissing, low growling, clicking, and sneezing. The North American opossum looked down from the tree, standing on a branch, using its tail for a kickstand.

Sasha was foot stomping and thumping. She snorted, honked, and screeched. Sasha nipped at the air, scratched the snow, and lunged at the tree. She beseeched the opossum for her heart. "Where is Loretta?" she asked, "Where?"

Virginia opossum scrambled down the tree and flashed an acorn at Sasha. Out of nowhere it had six more acorns. It juggled all seven high into the air, all the time jumping and clicking.

"Oh, Virginia opossum I want your acorns, I really do, but I have to find my heart. I may come back later." And with that she grabbed her knees, curled into a tight ball, and nodded off into the mystical.

Sasha floated in the mist. She looked down and saw Loretta in the forest. Loretta followed footprints in the snow, which were scattered everywhere. The footprints crossed each other and wound in circles.

Sasha saw Loretta enter the meadow. She walked toward that growing river in the aspens that Sasha had waded through. Lorette traipsed slowly through the deep snow until she reached the water, and there across the now-wide river from her, Sasha watched in repose.

"Okay, I tell you what I'll do," Sasha said to herself. "I'll offer myself so that I may rejoin Loretta, on the far side of the river." Sasha looked up. "You can consume me and bring us back together."

Sasha summoned all her strength and soared upward to standing. She whirled and gathered sticks from the wind. She wailed and crumpled leaves fell from her eyes. With a hop and shrill she summoned jackal fire from her paws and lit a blazing fire. She loomed higher.

"I will offer you myself as the finest delicacy, oh great moon, that you may become full and wise, that you may bring my heart back to me, across this great river. And with that she hopped high into the air and landed deep in the fire. Burn away the poison, burn the desire, burn my grasp on this world."

But her fur did not burn; her flesh did not alight. She felt cold instead of hot. Her bones shivered the chill of an icy wave.

"Why will I not burn! I offer myself to the fire! To the moon! To the sky!"

She stood again. Trembling. She fell with a splash. The river took her and swiftly washed her toward the other side, toward the far bank. Her breathing slowed, her blood pumped slower and slower, and her eyes closed forever. Loretta saw her out in the water and bawled into the night. She roared, ran through the clear, cold water and tried to wake her heart's heart. She threw her head back and wailed at the moon, and just at that moment, a wisp of white light spiraled out into the sky, swirling and swirling and swirling. Sasha evaporated upward.

The solid white moon changed its texture, filled with a new pattern, a design imprinted forever on its surface—the likeness of a rabbit shining from moon to earth, moving the waves of the ocean, the tides—a rhythm, a heartbeat—to be found washing against the shores of every continent, turning the wheel of time with every cycle, with every waxing and every waning.

Loretta remained under the sky and the stars and wanders still today among the aspens, spruces, and pines. She can be heard in the bellowing holler of winter storms and the rustling crackle of quaking leaves. She can be found near the wandering river, gazing into the moon's reflection in water, waiting for spring.

I You and You Me

Jim Richards

The problem with understanding is that it never happens. A spouse, a lover, a friend says, *I understand you*, but they don't. A pet looks at you with that look but has no clue. The soldier on her back, a boot on her chest, a barrel between her lips thinks she gets it, and so does the guy on the other side of the gun. I have seen two ants approach each other on the sidewalk and gesture with antennae for several minutes then scurry off in frustration. A goldfinch stood on my deck for an hour staring at the small crescent of feathers stuck to the window it collided with, contemplating glass? gravity? *It was stunned*, you say, and I would agree. I went out to explain, but the bird kept putting its tail toward me. You understand, right? You know what I mean when I say understanding never happens? That's what I'm afraid of, this certainty we have when we stand under the stars and say we understand—I you and you me.

Kate

Andrew Robin

My friend Kate has a tumor in her brain.
It's deep in there where they can't operate.
It's benign and growing slowly;
she says she just has to wait.
'Wait for what?' I say.
'For it to get too large,' she says,
'and I start to lose balance
or go blind in one eye.'
'And then what?' I say.
But we go quiet;
we've reached the crux of the truth,
it's a precipice from which
you can't step back.
So we sit a long time in that silence,
while the dying we all have to do hovers distantly,
hangs palely ahead of us in our separate skies
like a moon in the daylight.
So far away sometimes, it's barely a moon at all.
So close sometimes, you can almost
reach and touch it.

The Answer Is No

Dennis Lum

Your chair an eagle's nest.
You, propped by armrests, restless
in its worn contours, long pressed flat
by bony legs and seat.

Neurons misfire.
Connective tissue still delicate.
And yet your wings
ready themselves to sculpt waves in space.

Clear-eyed, hungry
to ride the draft   into clouds

                  evening sun

                        suspended in horizons

spying   then

           diving

        steel talons out   fast

                  faster

    than prey or foe   can flee—

The Answer Is No

No you do not want
to pray with the hospice chaplain;
you know soon you will
rise from the branch open wide

                your glory

                     and spring forth

burst the sound barrier   free even   from wing

        become in full   the royal azure

          caressing

              the eagle's maiden hunt.

Homecoming

Corey S. Pressman

here, at the beginning
of end of the viral invasion

i squat in the side yard
peering into my

hands, counting
silver linings

death does not wait long for us
we, running like mad

right into his outstretched
arms, nuzzling his skull

against ours
where have you been?

he whispers through tears
i thought you were lost

Homecoming

he says
holds us by the shoulders

at arm's length
my how you've grown

I Am Stillborn

Judith Mikesch McKenzie

The child I was supposed to be left the womb
  with unmoving lungs and silent heart
  and vanished into a stack of records
  and procedures.

My parents did not name him, my brother
  who never was, and there was no
  funeral, but in a house crowded
  with women, he was a presence.

The hoped-for, but unrealized. The
  unfulfilled wish.

There were things the iron will of our
  ancestors forbade us to speak of
  or acknowledge. In the high green
  hills where my parent's parents
lived, it was held true that the spirit of
  the stillborn child would be reborn
  in the body of the next-born.

Name the child the same, to invite the
       child back to the family, to entice
       it to leave the place beyond the
       veil and return to those
who yearn quietly for him.

Yet unnamed my brother was, and I
       the unwitting receptacle for his
       lost and wandering spirit which
never settled easy in me, he without
       a name.

Girl on Rocky Creek Bridge

Cecil Morris

She walks barefoot along the wide concrete
side wall of the old bridge that spans the gorge
where the creek spills out of land and into sea,
into a tumble of wave-beat rocks sixty feet
below the classical revival span, arches
beside and over one grand arch that holds
all tensions in check and bears the road bed
across the gap, 360 feet.
From the roadside turnout, the bridge looks grand
and the girl looks small, a tiny gymnast
on massive bridge's beam, a dinosaur
of architectural engineering,
an historic landmark and a slight girl,
maybe 16, maybe 20. She walks
across the wind, her skirt pressed to her legs,
the edges snapping, her blouse fluttering,
her hair like streaming flags. She holds her arms
up and out from her sides like a tightrope
walker, a sandal dangling from each hand
balancing beauty and danger, past
and present, daring the world with action.

Who Shall It Be!

Laura Wolf Benziker

The Summer House *really* was large. It was *twice* as large as Opal's family's town house in the city. It was *three* times as large as Cecelia's family's regular house in the college town. The Summer House had three levels, with high ceilings (not even counting the attic). Each level was narrower than the one below, but stacked up right at the middle, so it looked like a wedding cake, except blue. The Summer House was speckled with windows all shapes and sizes. Inside as you tramped about you might come face to face with a person-sized window on the third floor. You would peer down at the sea fathoms below and turn dizzy as a phonograph record. Or you might find yourself gazing out of a half moon window (divided peacock-tail-like by lines of lead) into the thick of a flowering tree. Or through an octagonal porthole from one room into another. In that case look or don't, but don't blame me.

Opal and Cecelia were cousins. Opal had nine years and Cecelia had eight. In June their parents rented The Summer House on the island. It was the same island as it was last June, and the same house also.

Cecelia arrived at The Summer House after a half-mile walk from the station, carrying her plaid train case and holding her mommy's hand. Her daddy was to arrive the next day, as he had imperative business to attend to. As Cecelia approached along the vaulted carriage path she saw a small brown-braided head appear in a second floor window (that was Opal) then disappear, for eleven seconds, then fly out the front door towards her. The cousins clasped wrists and spun on the new grass.

"Who shall it be!" squealed Opal

"Who shall it be!" piped Cecelia

After retrieving the train case Cecelia was bustled up the stairs into their shared room on the third floor by Opal, who had been bored already two days from waiting for her. They each received one twin bed, blue, with three pillows, ruffled, and a vanity with mirror to share between them.

The Summer House had a wrap-around porch which was most agreeable on the sunny days. Nailed to the center post of it was an ancient ship's figurehead. She was a lady of elm in flowing blue dress, amber tresses in briny disarray. With poise the figurehead stayed, shoulders thrown back, sublime bosom aloft, hand in place to shade her eyes as she scanned the sea for hazards. Here was one who knew her role and embodied it with dignity.

There were two mommies and they were both beautiful and they were Cecelia's and Opal's mommies and they were sisters with each other. There were two daddies, and one of them was tall and handsome and that was Opal's daddy.

Cecelia's mommy drifted through The Summer House in ivory frocks. Her penny-shaded curls tumbled down her back, and Cecelia thrilled to look up at them swaying when they would walk together. When Cecelia's mommy moved, her collarbones went first, and her slender hand last, lagging behind as if she were trailing it in the calm waters of a lagoon. She smiled often, a soft sad smile, and spoke rarely. When she spoke it was with a gentle voice bringing to mind a woodland doe.

Opal's mommy wore her dark hair clipped short and angled so that it curled just-right under her lovely ears. Every morning she circled her dusky eyes with black maquillage from a patterned tin. In the late sunset evenings at The Summer House she sat on a high barstool amid a proliferation of visiting grownups. She listened, and occasionally puffed from her long cigarette holder. At just the right moment she would speak just the right thing. She spoke with a deep and dark voice that hid far down inside it: a laugh. When guests heard it the laughs were shaken right out of them like a tablecloth swiped from underneath formal place settings!

There were two daddies and one of them was tall and handsome and that was Opal's daddy. There was one daddy who had to go to work almost all the time and that was Cecelia's daddy.

The mommies carried little silver canteens in their handbags, and these canteens they sipped at during the day when they weren't under the glance of admirers. The daddies poured their murky drink from a robust decanter which they shared, laughing in the library, tobacco smoke escaping into the hall. When Opal took the decanter from the high shelf she almost dropped it on the piano it was that heavy.

"We must try a taste," explained Opal, "for we are to be grownups one day."

Cecelia shuddered, then stamped her feet on the Turkish carpet to banish the thought from her head.

Opal sipped and made a face like falling in the sea in Green Land.

Cecelia sipped and made a face like falling in the sea in Ann Artica.

On a fog-soaked day *last* June, Cecelia had been sitting tucked up into a window nook when her mommy and Opal's daddy slipped into an empty room down the hall. Cecelia lingered, looking out the window at yellow-green vines creeping from the lilac tree onto the dormer. Funny noises began to emerge from the room. Though the noises weren't loud, they were of a kind of noise that made you want to go away from there. Cecelia did that.

During their regular lives (in the city, in the college town) Opal's family and Cecelia's family did like families with children ought to do: nurture, love, punish, ignore. At The Summer House, they only ignored. Bedtimes forgotten, freedom of kitchen and provisions (mostly cheese and olives, joy!), ramblings permissed.

In the evenings Opal and Cecelia would weave their way through the roomfuls of grownups. More guests arrived by the day, and now it was chock full. Cecelia skipped in saddle shoes behind Opal, who was always the leader. She turned her head to the hypnotic drawl of an old lady elegantly slouched, draped in peach-colored silk scarves. Cecelia had heard other guests refer to the lady as a famous poet. The poet sneaked a look at Cecelia and winked! Cecelia blushed pink and hurried on. Opal in her Mary Janes trotted through the maze of swishing hems and tweed trousers, through the glimmer of sparkling bead necklaces and gold watches on chains. She dodged a pool of spilled champagne, grabbed a crab cake from a tray, and flopped onto a velvet settee which had conspicuous cigarette burns. Cecelia sat next to her, straight-backed and google-eyed. They breathed quick and their eyes darted. A sandy-haired gentleman with round spectacles sauntered toward them with a smile. He nodded and lifted his highball glass. Opal jumped up, grabbed for the wrist of Cecelia who was smiling back at the man, and bolted. In the library they snatched up a wooden Parcheesi set, swiped chocolate truffles from an abandoned tray, and took the stairs two at a time up to the third floor. Along the dark corridor they coughed through dense fumes emanating from an open door. Passing they saw a vaporous gentleman lying facedown on stained sheets, snoring like a walrus. At the end of the hallway they passed through the doorway of their own room, and thumped it shut with a satisfying click. "That's enough of that!" said Opal.

Next morning Cecelia and Opal woke *hours* before the grownups. Downstairs they creaked open the icebox to gather green olives and Cam and Bear for breakfast, which they laid out neatly on great husks of French bread left over. As they crunched, large crumbs showered down on the rumpled linen draping the mahogany table. Sated and sore-jawed, they wiped their mouths on the edge of the tablecloth, retired to the library and flopped upon full tummies on the Turkish carpet. They settled in to read picture books, and talk and sketch in a notebook they had found on a bookshelf, while the grandfather clock ticked imposingly and the stale air of the past evening settled into the pine floor boards.

Presently Cecelia grew bored. She rose, and ambled through drawing room, dining room, hallway, foyer. On the wall in the foyer was a gilt-frame mirror, very old, a fishes eye one. It was too high up the wall for Cecelia to look in, so she dragged a heavy chair from its spot in the drawing room. Clambering up she viewed her own self. In the mirror it appeared that she was ten feet distant as opposed to only the three. She stood precariously on tiptoes, arms flung wide, narrow chest thrust forward, and put on her face an expression of pride and wisdom. She held it for as long as she could, her image wobbling against the still background of The Summer House, silent.

She then hopped down, declining to return the chair to its place, and went out to the porch to speak to the figurehead. This she did only when alone, without even Opal.

"Mommy" she said, gazing up at the smooth white chin,

"There are too many things. I want to be blind like you, and with my eyes open, so no one will know"

Secret shared, she made her way back to the library and Opal, to while away the hours.

If it weren't for being with Opal, Cecelia would have been afraid to wander. Opal on the other hand, would *not* have been afraid to wander *without* Cecelia, but it was of course *so boring* to wander alone.

Cecelia and Opal skipped down the shore path hand-in-hand. Cecelia, on the interior side, brushed her face amongst the wild ocean rose bushes, not minding a few scratches for the pleasure of the smell. Opal, on the exterior side, glided her eyes along the golden horizon of sunset, the dark humped islands looming and beckoning from the bay. And the machinations of people: iron pilings drilled into rounded flanks of pink granite, colonies of sea life dredged up from the inky depths (those of lesser value left to flop and rot and stink on the rocky beaches), cobbled walkways, bronze plaques, benches, whitewashed gazebos sitting bold and complacent, as if the island were purposely designed to host the throngs, and why would it be any other way?

Cecelia, letting her head tip back in fragrant bliss, was first to see it. The violet orb hovered, vibrating above them at the height of a tall oak. Cecelia yanked on Opal's hand and pulled her still. They froze, and watched as the orb began to move steadily through the air. Opal whispered,

"Who shall it be!"

The luminous sphere floated over a sprawling lawn with tennis court and marble fountain. It moved toward the mansion lording over

the lawn. The mansion had a feature that Cecelia and Opal had no-
ticed in many of the houses on the island, and that was a small round
window near the top. Most people wouldn't have even noticed it. They
trained their eyes on that round window because *they* knew what was
going to happen. The orb moved toward the window and for a flash
they saw it reflected, violet white hot, and through it went! Cecelia and
Opal stood for a moment, a temporary blaze in their eyes, then turned
away and continued to skip down the shore path toward the town.

During summer there were *too many* people. The lush blooming
greenage was crimped in by horse-and-carts, motorcars, rowdy hoards
singing bellowing smoking hassling. Steamships with their bedrock-
shaking honks. Great Danes, fine dames, dashing rakes, saucy ladies,
jaded servants, faux-jade antique hustlers, swashbucklers, bicyclists,
ice cream kiosks, carts jammed with stoneware jugs smuggled from
already debarked boats and conveyed to those with the scoop and the
dough, tents under which you could buy post cards, snake oil, tiny
pewter boats, amateur oil paintings, or have your fortune told by a
turbaned lady of mystery.

Cecelia and Opal tramped up the path from the shore to the
main street and they were in the thick of it.

"There are too many *people*," said Opal.

"The *island* says so," said Cecelia.

As they neared the village green the sun pulled a ruffled indigo
coverlet over itself. Gaslights were lit one by one. A string band played
chanteys to which a trio of curly-haired wenches kicked their heels
and swung their skirts, flashing scalloped bloomers. Cecelia and Opal
walked at a glacial pace, with big wide eyes.

A feral hoard of grownups pranced on the village green to the
rhythm of the fiddle, accordion, and drum. They whooped and clapped

and stumbled and sloshed grog with not a single care. Then Opal saw him. She nudged Cecelia.

"Who shall it be!" Cecelia whispered.

He was a tall, thin man. Dark hair and long curved moustaches, and he appeared stricken. Stricken absolutely from the ranks of humanity. He stood still as a mast in the churning sea of grownups. Still as a mast, and his eyes glowed violet. Opal and Cecelia locked him in their gaze and concurrently shrunk themselves back into the shadow of the brick building.

This chosen man drifted back dead-like through the crowd, propped up tall and staring into nowhere. It was as though he were being reeled in by a hidden puppeteer all in black. He receded farther into the dimmest reaches of the park. Cecelia and Opal both swore afterward that dark green leaves had sprouted from the sides of his head. Soon all that could be seen of him were glowing eyes in the swaying branches of lilac at the edge of the woods. Presently the lights blinked out.

Cecelia and Opal turned and stared at one another. Thrill is a Fright is a Scare is a Light, their eyes volleyed. Fright is a Scare is a Light. Flicker, flicker, flicker, Smite! The shadow in which they stood, without warning loomed corporeal as a huge man stepped up at them. His beard had bits of things stuck to it and he grinned and breathed heavy and foul through the many black spaces where the teeth ought to be. His green eyes were drawn wide and they could see the white part around the edges and it was horrible.

He opened his arms to corner them and spread his thick fingers in presentation.

"Pretty girls! You like toys? I have a toy for you!"

Quick as a weasel the man pulled down his trousers to expose a mass of black hair and some lumps of pink flesh that were the worst things that Cecelia and Opal saw in their entire whole lives.

Opal grabbed Cecelia's wrist, ducked under the dreadful arm, and ran swift as a springbok across the street, through the crowd of dancing grownups, through the tents, through the swaying lilacs, through the dark woods of bark and branches and fronds and other trustworthy things, onto the shore path. Only then did Opal surrender Cecelia's wrist. The girls went limp and tumbled to their knees. Gradually they found their breath and brought it down to the quiet path with them. Then they stood, hand-in-hand, and took the shore path back toward The Summer House. They rounded the secret corner of rose bushes that led into the garden. From the bottom of the garden looking up the sloped lawn, The Summer House seemed to be hanging in the sky before them. Its many windows glowed amber and strawberry against the indigo firmament. Cecelia and Opal both noticed, at the exact same moment, a window they had never seen before. A small, round window at the very top, at the attic it must have been. As they stood, with the solemnity of orphans, the violet orb took a straight path to the small attic window. With a white hot flash it entered.

The cousins clasped wrists and turned in a slow circle. One time, two times, three times. Then they let go and flopped onto the soft damp grass. Opal rolled over to Cecilia and curled up snug, draping her arm protectively across her cousin's small ribcage. They slept, and the lilacs swayed.

When a Woman Becomes a Tree, a Forest Becomes a Fire

Laura Ruby

A woman writes that when she was a girl, her mother taught her to cross off the days of the month on a calendar. Red for blood.

Another writes that some months, the blood didn't come. Some months, it came twice.

A woman writes that cramps would rack her body for hours, leave her for dead on the bathroom floor.

A woman writes that the first time her blood came, her father called her a whore.

Sick of her own treacherous flesh, a woman turns herself into a doll—lock-limbed, oblivious, perfect.

A woman testifies about her rape. It was a stranger. He left her for dead on the bathroom floor.

A woman testifies about her rape. It was her uncle. She got pregnant. At fourteen.

A woman testifies about her rape. There were six of them. She was twelve. She'll never carry a child.

A man on the highest court in the land was accused of rape. In his defense, he offered a calendar.

A woman turns herself into a pair of oven mitts. Or a tea cup. A trivet. A shaker of salt. Salt.

A woman writes about an abortion. It saved her life.

A woman writes that she gave the baby up for adoption.

A woman writes that people came and took her baby. She never found the child.

A woman writes that she loves all her children and wants to love herself.

A woman writes that she is a person, but she doesn't seem sure.

A woman turns herself into the sound of heels tapping through a deserted parking garage.

A woman writes that her boyfriend won't wear condoms because they don't feel natural.

A woman writes that her boyfriend flushed her birth control pills down the toilet because they just weren't natural.

When a Woman Becomes a Tree, a Forest Becomes a Fire

A woman writes that when her boyfriend found out she was pregnant, he kicked her down the stairs.

A woman writes about the twins that died at 22 weeks. Carrying them to term could have killed her. Her sorrow almost did.

A woman writes about giving birth to a dead baby.

A woman writes about giving birth to a dead baby.

A woman writes about giving birth to a dead baby.

A woman turns herself into a ghost you can only see out of the corner of your eye. A scrim of clouds over the moon. Steam writhing over your coffee.

A woman writes about her daughter giving birth to a dead boy. Her daughter died of sepsis.

A woman writes about the stroke she had during childbirth.

A woman writes that giving birth nearly tore her in half. For weeks, she couldn't use the toilet without passing out.

A woman writes that the United States has the highest maternal death rate of all wealthy nations. The story is killed.

A man writes about how much he worships his mother.

When a Woman Becomes a Tree, a Forest Becomes a Fire

The man's wife is also a mother, but he ditched her for a younger version.

Athena turns Medusa into a Gorgon, who then turns men into stone.

A woman writes that she wanted to get her tubes tied but the doctor refused. Her future husband might object. It's only natural.

A woman writes that thousands of women in the United States have been sterilized against their will.

A man writes: Hysteria.

When the other gods ask who, exactly, Athena's trying to punish, not even the owl can give a straight answer.

A woman writes that she didn't know she was pregnant.

A woman writes that she didn't know she was pregnant.

A person writes that they didn't know they were pregnant.

A man writes: Impossible.

A woman turns herself into a mirror. A razor. A line of cocaine.

A woman writes about the sudden pain, the rush of blood and tissue into the toilet, the dizziness, the grief/relief, the tears, what-could-have-beens.

A woman is jailed for having a miscarriage.

A woman is jailed for having a miscarriage.

A woman is jailed for having a miscarriage.

A woman turns herself into a tumor. A woman turns herself into a heart attack.

Another man writes: I'm sympathetic, but a uterus is a uterus. One must weigh a mother's interests against the interests of the fetus.

More men write about weights, about interests.

A woman writes that she is interested in being a person.

Sick of her lock-limbed embrace, Pygmalion prays his ivory doll becomes flesh—yielding, oblivious, perfect.

A woman on the highest court in the land grew up in a radical sect in which wives submit to the judgment of their husbands. She's content to force everyone else to submit to her.

A man writes, You can be a person or a mother. Your choice. Wait. Scratch that. You can be a nun. Wait.

The woman on the highest court in the land said pregnancy is no hardship. Men listen because she's a woman and a woman would know.

When a Woman Becomes a Tree, a Forest Becomes a Fire

A man writes that a woman can be a judge if she judges other women.

A woman writes, Fuck it, I'd rather be a tree.

A woman fetals inside an orange. She hides there for weeks before a man picks and eats her.

A newspaper runs a story about a girl hunted by a rapist. Just as the rapist caught her by the hair, her skin roughened, thickened, leaves shot from her fingertips, her mouth yawned into a nesting hole for squirrels.

A woman writes about her rape. She said the rapist was the president.

The rapist president rammed the rapist judge and the doll-eyed hand-maid onto the highest court in the land. People are content to write about it.

A group of women establish their own wood in Canada. Another group plants themselves in Washington State. A third takes over the Black Forest.

Tiny groves sprout everywhere.

A man writes that it's impossible to know which trees are trees and which trees are women.

A man writes something-something-family, something-something-values, something-something-God.

A man writes that tree-women are witches. Dangerous. Unnatural.

A man writes that there ought to be a law.

A man writes that women who become trees should be chopped down and carved into cradles.

A man writes that all the trees should burn.

A grinning man is photographed perched on a stump.

The grinning man says, This is what Jesus wants.

A man sets fire to a forest and cheers at the blaze.

Deep in the earth, tree roots twine, testify.

Miles away, in Indiana, a stand of aspens curls green fists. Through a courthouse roof, they punch for the sun—leaves quaking, newly born.

Middle Aged Couple, Too Restless to Sleep

Tom C. Hunley

Mating song of cicadas
seeps through silence.
Animal noise, noise of the day
opening its jaws.

Sunrise over vibrating wind in leaves.

And though our bodies ache separately
our dazed half-dreams merge.
Music and silence fuse into a memory
that the wind, in love with motion, carries away.

Thunder, lightning, beautiful together.
That quick, the song vanishes.

The Other House

Claudia Putnam

I lived ten years in my family's first house, a tiny, ancient Cape-Cod crammed with furniture and increasingly crowded with children. After we moved around the corner, to the house where our parents divorced, we always called the first place "the other house." We still refer to it that way, 45 years later, during Thanksgivings in the "new" home, also a small 1770s Cape, where we spent the rest of our childhoods. I guess this means: even if your tall and handsome father came home drunk *every* night, belt-whipped you when not lying atop you boozily protesting his love, locked your pretty, cowardly mother in the cellar, even if the house was haunted, inimically, we still pine for that time BCDE, before the current divorce era.

Our house was small, too, but somehow spacious inside, its 12-foot ceilings and Victorian nooks accommodating even the furniture that had felt out of place in our first home, which you loved and I did not. Where we had lived for 10 years, half our marriage. This Victorian house, in a new town, was a rental, unhaunted despite its age. Its responsibilities did not weigh upon us. One dog, two cats died there. We grieved, but were buoyed by the mystery of the happiness we found in that house. The sex amazing—rough, adventurous, attuned—finally. We exclaimed, to friends, to each other, over our happiness, this discovery, our physical delight in each other despite the familiarity, the hard years behind us. How lucky we were, in our marriage, in this adorable town, this cute house. Five years in that house.

I feared our luck would turn when our landlord sold the house. We found another cute Victorian, only a little haunted, just little larger, around the corner. This time we bought, and though we said we were thrilled, I felt queasy. We hadn't done well, overall, with external stressors. Moves are stressful. The house would need work. Though it was larger, it was less accommodating in its design. Our pets did not like it as much. For weeks the cat went back to the old house.

Our luck did turn. It took a while to see this. Your misery as strange and mysterious as our happiness in the previous house. I don't expect to know what caused it. The undeniability of aging? The departure of your erections? The deaths of the dogs? The disaster with the plumbing? It wasn't a dream house for either of us. Now we owned it, would probably die in it. Meaning, this was it. Not a bad place, not at all—friends who had never been to the rental house cooed over its cuteness—but now it was settled. Things, our circumstances, would not get any better.

We sold our furniture. Bought new stuff. I was constantly painting, rearranging.

After four years, this house we bought in the town, in the neighborhood, we loved became the house of our divorce. We began speaking of the previous place, the house around the corner, as "the other house." The house where we were other, where it was other than it is now. You thought the sex was good in that house, too, right? You thought we were lucky, in the other house. You thought me difficult then, bipolar writer, but we loved each other in the other house. Right?

How homesick I feel for the houses of otherness, of indecision, of futures still open. Those old houses just around the corner.

What We Look Forward To

Jim Richards

Wasn't tomorrow nice,
the way it hovered before us
like a helium balloon unable to rise
for the weight of its string but not

sinking either? Tomorrow was a room
empty but ready for guests with tables full of food
and drink, cushioned chairs arranged, dim light,
music coming from nowhere. It was

a singular event anticipated, a child
standing on a runway, looking up at
the rising jets, an empty picture frame
given as a gift. Honestly, it was you—

your vague face, your voice, your scent
after a shower. Tomorrow was all of this.
But terrible we have had to turn around,
and what we look forward to now is yesterday.

Lion Hunt
—Eugène Delacroix, 1855

Peter J. Grieco

The effect is inseparable from its massive size
the viewer dwarfed & abutted,
forms crowding close & struggling
to rise, every inch filled with matter & agony
proximity, entanglement. Detachment
is not its subject, but oiliness
& carnality, everything by excess
all or none, half the canvas gone up
in smoke, beheaded, & broken-

necked. What's left is fantasy mixed with shock
the "stuff" of color, the muscle tightening
power of figures prone, improbably
twisted through multiple extensions
to create a "turbulence sown together"
then torn apart again
at the threads, until the lion
wins.

The Astronomer

John Peter Beck

Somehow, St. Dominic
became the patron saint

of all astronomers, a mystery
even to the Vatican

Observatory itself. Dominic,
though certainly a good man,

seems to have had
no special drive or desire

to understand as much
about the heavens

as heaven. I would choose
another to be our patron saint,

even one of his same Dominican order,
Giordano Bruno.

The Astronomer

Burned at the stake for his heresy,
Bruno posited that Earth was not

The center of the universe
a starry firmament

set in time and place, ordained
and cemented by God.

The fate of Bruno,
and many more like him,

was decided by men
who claimed they spoke

to God, for God, as God
and they called Bruno the heretic!

Every night, I marvel it is my job
to stare up at the celestial swirl—

I would do it for free. When day ends,
perhaps both St. Dominic and I should

say an extra prayer for Giordano Bruno.
I am sure that a loving God

could not condemn a man
who wanted so deeply

to understand
the grand dance,

to track the movement divine
of this night's sky.

Beg the Question

Maria Berardi

—for Joel

Which is stranger,
that serendipitous, synchronistic things

happen according to some larger plan
which we know only partially, imperfectly—

or that we have such minds
as to create such a thought?

If free will
does not exist

then it is *all*
the hot stove and the hand.

An odd God. An imaginary friend,
a real friendship.

The holy *maybe*
and the holy conjunction *and*.

Doubt your faith,
and then doubt your doubt;

creation created, creation creating,
wonder. Akin to salvation.

I seem to have made a pact, years ago,
to follow the meaning-making

mystery of my mind,
to faithfully follow the yarn I myself am spinning.

Oona in the Altogether

Dallas Crow

Oona Chadwick had often insisted to anyone who would listen that she was to be buried wearing her pearl necklace. What no one had expected of Oona—long-standing member and three-time president of the Junior League, and widow of local luminary, former mayor, and one-time Republican candidate for congress Gordon Chadwick—was that her will would declare she was to be buried *only* in her pearls.

What do you do when your mother wants to be buried in her birthday suit? The Chadwick children argued.

Gordon Jr., a real estate broker, said if that's what she wanted, then it should be done. No one would be hurt. The dead can't be embarrassed. And nowhere in the will did it say she wanted an open casket. Bury her naked in a closed casket and no one would be the wiser.

His sister, Ruth, insisted the open casket was implied—what would be the point of being buried in the nude if no one knew?—and argued that her mother must have been suffering from dementia, though she had never said that before and couldn't come up with a single other symptom. She was apoplectic, inconsolable, as if the very foundation of her world were falling apart.

Though I didn't say anything right away, I sided with Gordon. If God truly is omniscient, He's seen all of us in the altogether (basically all the time). There was nothing about Oona Chadwick's withered 78 year old body that would titillate or appall Him. It was unusual for sure, unprecedented in my experience, but it was all the same to me. It wasn't like I hadn't seen other unclothed corpses. It would actually mean a little less work for me, less handling of the body since I didn't have to dress her and prepare her for display, though I had no plans to offer them a discount based on that.

They both had seemed anguished enough by their mother's request that I didn't expect them to be discussing it with others, so I was stunned when I got home from work and Rhoda asked me if it was true that Oona was going to be buried in the nude. It was more surprising to me that she had heard about it than that it was what Oona wanted, and like I said, that's the first time I have ever heard of such a request. I quickly tried to do the math in my head. Rhoda isn't close to Gordon or Ruth, and you would think Ed Lanier, Oona's lawyer and her husband's longtime partner at Chadwick Lanier, would keep such a thing confidential. Plus, it's not like Rhoda and Ed travel in the same circles, even if he was gabbing.

"Where did you hear that?"

"So it's true," she said, a coy smile on her face. "Oona Chadwick! Who woulda thunk it?"

An hour later, in the middle of dinner (pork chops and salad), I got a call from Steve Benson, owner, editor, and chief reporter of the *Daily Mirror*, wanting to know the same thing.

"No comment," I said.

"So it's true."

"No comment, Steve. I never comment on the specifics of arrangements. I announce the date and time, what families want in lieu of flowers, that kind of thing. If you want to know more, you've got to go to the family."

He was equally unhelpful when I asked what led him to call me. "Can't reveal my sources, Sid. You know that. I don't even know what kind of story I could or would run if you confirmed it."

The next morning I got a call from the *Free Press* downstate, and in the afternoon, I took calls from *USA Today* and the *New York Times*. They all wanted to know the same thing, and I gave them all the same useless response. The reporter from the *Times* said they had two accounts of similar instances, one in New Orleans and one in Oregon, and if they had a third they would have a trend story.

"Can you run it with just two examples?" I asked.

"Nope. Then it's just a coincidence."

It gave me a funny feeling. All this talk was going on, a rumor (never mind how accurate it was) spreading wider and faster than I ever could have imagined. The cliché would be that it was spreading like wildfire, only that doesn't begin to capture the speed and distance, and a fire is highly visible. It felt to me like a tunneling thing, like an extended family of massive groundhogs or moles working just beneath the surface, and threatening to erupt at any time and who knows where? At this point it was merely gossip—invisible, as likely or more likely to be untrue than true—but without warning, apparently, it could burst forth as national news—confirmed, factual, part of the permanent record (however trivial) of the entire nation.

I locked my office door, poured myself a drink, and called Gordon.

The man I reached was not happy with me at all—to put it mildly. He had been contacted by the same reporters, and he had assumed that hungry for a little bit of glory, I had tipped them off. After a while I talked him down and convinced him of the truth, that I had not initiated anything, and that I hadn't given the hounds anything more than a *no comment*. His anger transformed rapidly to an inarticulate befuddlement. "But who...but why...what would they hope...?" Each partial sentence drifted off into silence before he would try another that he couldn't complete.

I told him that I figured there were four of us who knew initially, and if he and I hadn't told anyone...at which point he admitted he had told his wife. Nothing wrong with that, but I took the opportunity to tell him I had given my own wife a *no comment*.

"Well, you're a better man than I," he said.

"Probably not," I said. "It's the kind of thing you should share with your spouse. In any case," I added, "unless it's Greta" (his wife), "it's got to be either Ruth or Ed."

There was a long pause on the line, and then he said, "You know, when your mother dies at the age my mother did, the way she did" (a heart attack in her sleep at home), "aside from the normal grieving, there should be a fair amount of comfort—that she died quickly, that she didn't suffer, that she didn't have to experience ongoing deterioration and dementia or institutionalization, that she saw both her children in happy marriages, economically secure, grandchildren who didn't dye their hair funny colors or pierce body parts that weren't meant to be pierced, but here I am, wondering who my mother was, and who her friends and family really are. Why did she want to be buried in the nude so badly that she put it in her will, and who would then go spread this around and why? I don't know, Sid. I just want to mourn; I don't want to have to ask all these questions."

As it turned out, none of the papers ran the story. The funeral went off without a hitch—at least as far as I could tell. The coffin was closed, attendance was about what you would expect, and there was no untoward whispering that I could detect, no rude comments that I overheard. Gordon said Ruth, Ed, and Greta all denied spilling the beans. In the end, it's a mystery. I would love to know why Oona Chadwick's final wish was to be buried in nothing but her pearl necklace, and I wonder who started to spread the word and why, but it's not my style or place to press the issue, and as best as I can tell, no one but Oona could answer the first question, and whoever knows the answer to the second one isn't telling. My hunch is that it was her daughter, Ruth, that she was so appalled the only way she could process it was aloud. I bet after she acceded that afternoon to Gordon and her mom's wishes, she went home and worked the phone lines like nobody's business, a modern, almost civilized form of wailing, maybe even getting back at her mother, not just for this but for who knows what else?

Trumpeting

Leonardo Chung

months pass by,
and with them follow celebrations. the ones
in the elementary school classrooms, i mean.
stiff with new crisp trousers,
toes squirming in too-tight shoes,
the other classmates apportioned their morsels
but not with
me. goodies snatched by eager hands, but when
i outreached a finger—or maybe two—
i was forced into being an untouchable,
the snacks were some foreign currency.

months passed by,
chaperoning my birthday. my mother
didn't know about the cupcake customs conducted.
she left me at the front entrance with a wave and a "have fun!"

arriving in the classroom with a tray full of waves and "have fun!"s,
my beaming expression received no reciprocation,
except my teacher's gift:

Trumpeting

a brittle-lead pencil dropped off at my desk
covered with a scratched, peeling wrapper
with an accompanying smile
but at that moment
the barrier of stitching my mouth shut
while the arrows of "you have broken english" attacked
was released. an actual thought of me
encased in this wrapper.

what potential
the pencil was for me—do you see? brittle though, but
my thoughts could be voiced; useful to me
as when elephants trumpet of elation.
it is speech, but not spoken, traced in stone-grey, fragile lead.
open to interpretation, life-altering letters.

and when a million questions flutter in my mind like
birds off a telephone pole, i reach for a notepad and the delicate
        wooden trumpet—
creating unspoken words with it like a lively elephant,
letting the lead dust fly.

Ars Poetica In Review

Julia Hands

I want to hand it to you when it's still raw and beating,
slick and dripping.

Too hot to touch without oven mitts. The skin translucent,
ugly and loose, tentacles waving.

When it's pale and sketched out, the lines not holding together,
the eraser marks on the page.

When the pencil has just lifted, when the pen ink is still stuck
to the last letter of the last word stroked.

It's like the turkey before Thanksgiving. "All I Want For Christmas"
        played in September.
Your parents in bed.

I want to give you the me unprepared, so underdressed I haven't pulled
on my skin or trimmed my pubes.

This thing is sweaty and hairy, last night's make up still smudged
        under its eyelids.
It's unpretentious, untamed,

not even enough to be un. It has just plopped out of me
and I want to share it with you.

I don't want to hold it on my own.

Lilac Time

Joanne Esser

One evening we open our doors
and catch the scent of lilacs
strong in the air, surprising us.

We've been waiting for so long,
through dark afternoons,
snow turned gritty and gray,
through week after week of chill.

Its power transforms:
our mood, the air, the whole
neighborhood bursting purple, pink,
clumps of color within the new green.

Inhale. It's time now
for deeper breaths, longer strides,
the compulsion to move toward water,
as if we have been thirsty for all
these months. A loosening of shoulders
that have been clenched against our necks.

Lilac Time

They're turning on the rose garden fountain.
Art cars line up to parade,
sound a car horn concerto.
Spray painters make a new mural
on the white brick on Lyndale Avenue.

A hundred women and men—
toddlers to grannies—
salute the sun in unison on the grass.

A flotilla of canoes paddles
the giant sun puppet across the lake;
a team dressed in red raises it high.
We sing as it lifts. Some of us cry.
Though we witness it every year,
the sight of that triumphant return

restores what's been in hibernation,
releases cautious joy, the kind
only puppets, stilts and flowers provoke.

My kitchen faces east. Thick sun
like golden syrup floods in
through the glass door, spills
across the floor, leaks a puddle all the way
into the dining room.

Lilac Time

Soon I will go into the yard,
gather clusters of the small blossoms
from the bush, collect the fragrance
that started it all.

This Poem Writes Itself

David A. Goodrum

Though my plan is for you to write it.
There's an image in my mind's eye
smeared with dripping rain,
or tears if you lean that way,
an ekphrastic challenge,
and, like a god, give you four words as prompts:
Live.   Learn.   Love.   Leave.

Now improvise:

Contributors

Two of **Diane Averill's** books, *Branches Doubled Over With Fruit*, published by the University of Florida Press, and *Beautiful Obstacles*, published by Blue Light Press of Iowa, were finalists for the Oregon Book Award in Poetry, and her third book, *Among Pearls Hatching*, was published by Dancing Moon Press. She has been published in many anthologies and literary magazines including *Bloomsbury Review*, *Carolina Quarterly*, *Clackamas Literary Review*, *Midwest Quarterly*, *Poetry Northwest*, *Tar River Poetry*, and *The Carnegie Mellon-Anthology of Poetry*. Her most recent publications can be found in *Santa Clara Review* and *Mom Egg Review*. She taught English and poetry writing workshops at Clackamas Community College in Oregon City, OR, until retirement.

Naomi Azriel is a Bay Area based bilingual poet, queer & feminist activist and Jungian analyst. She grew up as the first of seven children in a religious family in Israel. In the US, she performed her work with the dyke erotica collective Dirty Ink. In both her clinical and poetic work, she reaches for complex interior spaces in which the fury of disillusionment and the sweetness of enchantment can coincide. Having had her heart broken by both her countries, she has been aiming to beam herself on a ray of dark matter into a wormhole between languages, between worlds, between the imaginary and the real. Her work can be found or is forthcoming from *Jung Journal*, *Barnacle Goose*, *BarBar*, *Gone Lawn*, *Closed Eye Open*, and *Red Noise Collective* as well as Israeli literary journals *Bita'on* and *Kol HeHamon*.

Heather Bartos has had essays in *Fatal Flaw*, *Stoneboat Literary Journal*, *HerStry*, and elsewhere, and upcoming in *McNeese Review*. Her flash fiction has appeared in *The Closed Eye Open*, *Peregrine*, *Orca*, *Santa Barbara Literary Journal*, and other publications, and won first place in the 2022 *Baltimore Review* Micro Lit Contest. She has also had short stories in *Ponder Review*, *Bridge Eight*, *Relief: A Journal of Art and Faith*, and elsewhere.

Nathan Bas is a Clackamas Community College and Portland State University graduate with publications in *Polaris* and the *Clackamas Literary Review*. He resides in Oregon City, OR, working as a pet-sitter and poem fiddler.

Scott Beard has a B.A. in Creative Writing and an M.A. in Curriculum and Instruction from Wichita State University. His fiction has appeared in over a dozen publications. He and his wife live with their dog, Drake, and their cat, Lucy, in Franklin, TN. He teaches English at Williamson College.

John Peter Beck is a professor in the labor education program at Michigan State University where he co-directs a program that focuses on labor history and the culture of the workplace, Our Daily Work/Our Daily Lives. "The Astronomer" is part of a larger series, *The Work of Saints*, which explores the intersection of occupations and the Catholic patron saints assigned to them. His poetry has been published in a number of journals including *The Seattle Review*, *Another Chicago Magazine*, *The Louisville Review*, and *Passages North*, among others.

Laura Wolf Benziker is a parent and small business owner making a messy go of it in Portland, ME. She is inspired by the subtle horrors of everyday life. Her work has appeared or is forthcoming in *Lit 202* and *The Bookends Review.*

Maria Berardi's poems appear online, in print, in university journals, meditation magazines, newspapers, and art galleries.

Ahimsa Timoteo Bodhrán is author of *Archipiélagos*; *Antes y después del Bronx: Lenapehoking*; and *South Bronx Breathing Lessons*; editor of the international queer Indigenous issue of *Yellow Medicine Review*; and co-editor of the Native dance/movement/performance issue of *Movement Research Performance Journal.* He has been a Sitka Center for Art & Ecology and Caldera Arts Center resident in the territories of the Confederated Tribes of Siletz Indians, Grand Ronde, Warm Springs, and Paiute. He believes more people should know the life-work of Elizabeth Woody, and find ways to center and support Indigenous Oregon writers.

Devon Borkowski is a writer, artist, and actor from the New Jersey Pine Barrens. She graduated from Rutgers New Brunswick class of 2022, with a BFA in Visual Arts. Her poetry and short stories have appeared in *The Dillydoun Reveiw*, *The Closed Eye Open*, and *Room Magazine.*

Tessa Broadie is a 21 year old student at Clackamas Community College living in Oregon City, OR. She enjoys making art, jewelry, and music.

Paul Brownsey lives in Scotland and is a former member of the Philosophy faculty at Glasgow University. His book, *His Steadfast Love and*

Other Stories, was published by Lethe Press, NJ, received a starred review in *Publishers Weekly*, and was a finalist in the Lambda Literary Awards. An earlier story by him was published in *Clackamas Literary Review* in Vol. XXII, 2018.

Joseph Byrd's work has appeared in *Fatal Flaw, South Florida Poetry Journal, DIAGRAM*, and forthcoming work in *WAXING & WANING* and *Tilted House*. He's a 2023 Pushcart Prize nominee, and was in the StoryBoard Chicago cohort with Kaveh Akbar. An Associate Artist in Poetry under Joy Harjo at the Atlantic Center for the Arts, he is on the Reading Board for *The Plentitudes*.

David Capps is a philosophy professor and poet who lives in New Haven, CT. He is the author of four chapbooks: *Poems from the First Voyage* (The Nasiona Press, 2019), *A Non-Grecian Non-Urn* (Yavanika Press, 2019), *Colossi* (Kelsay Books, 2020), and *Wheatfield with a Reaper* (Akinoga Press, forthcoming).

Leonardo Chung is a young aspiring writer who has attended several programs such as Iowa Young Writers' Studio, Sewanee Young Writers' Conference, and Juniper Summer Writing Institute. His work has been previously accepted by *Sheila-Na-Gig, Sweet Lit, Rigorous, Vermilion, riverSedge*, and others. He is the founder and editor of *Clepsydra Literary and Art Magazine*.

Dallas Crow has recently had work in *Aethlon: The Journal of Sports Literature, Florida Review, Flyfish Journal*, and *Louisiana Literature*. He teaches high school English and photography in Minnesota.

Tom Cullerton, an Oregon native, is retired from a thirty-five year career as a teacher for Portland Public Schools. Tom began writing poetry in the 70s, but took an extended pause while teaching full time. His poems have appeared in *The Oregonian* and the *North Coast Squid.*

Allison A. deFreese is a part-time instructor in Clackamas Community College's English Department and leads literary translation workshops for the Oregon Society of Translators and Interpreters. Her translation of Carolina Esses's book *Winter Season* is forthcoming from Entre Ríos Books (Seattle) in August of 2023.

Steve Deutsch is poetry editor of *Centered Magazine* and is poet in residence at the Bellefonte Art Museum. Steve was nominated three times for the Pushcart Prize. His Chapbook, *Perhaps You Can*, was published in 2019 by Kelsay Press. His full length books, *Persistence of Memory* and *Going, Going, Gone*, were published by Kelsay. *Slipping Away* will be published this spring. *Brooklyn* was awarded the Sinclair Poetry Prize from Evening Street Press and will also be published this spring.

Merridawn Duckler is a writer from Oregon, an installation artist, curator, and the author of three books, most recently *Misspent Youth* (rinky dink press.) New work in *Seneca Review, Posit, Plume,* and *Painted Bride Quarterly.* Winner of the Beulah Rose Poetry Contest from *Smartish Pace.* She's an editor at *Narrative* and the philosophy journal *Evental Aesthetics.*

Emily Eddins's poetry, creative nonfiction, and short fiction have appeared in publications such as *After the Pause, The Willow Review,*

The Louisville Review, The Penmen Review, Perceptions Magazine, The Toad Suck Review, Forge, Euphony Journal, Front Porch, The Cape Rock, The Round, Visitant Lit, Voices de la Luna, Edison Literary Review, Third Wednesday, and others. Her humorous essay collection, *Altitude Adjustment*, reached the Top Five in the Amazon Kindle Hot New Releases section for 90-minute short biographies. Emily's career includes time spent as a speechwriter, a journalist, and an editor. She holds a BA from Vanderbilt University, an MA from Georgetown University, and has studied creative writing at both Georgetown University and Stanford University. She lives in Northern California with her husband and three children.

Dean Engle is a writer and educator from the San Francisco Bay Area. He has been published in *Toyon Literary Magazine, Transfer Magazine, Brushfire Journal, the Ana, Santa Ana River Review, Great Lakes Review*, and *New Plains Review*, with an upcoming flash piece in *On the Run*. He's currently teaching intro to English at the community college level. In his spare time he enjoys watering his cactus and making soup!

Joanne Esser is the author of the poetry collection *Humming At The Dinner Table*, the chapbook *I Have Always Wanted Lightning*, and the forthcoming *All We Can Do Is Name Them*, (Fernwood Press, 2023). Recent work appears in *I-70 Review, Echolocation*, and *Wisconsin Review*. She earned an MFA from Hamline University and has been a teacher of young children for over forty years.

Writer and journalist **Carolina Esses** was born in Buenos Aires and lives in Bariloche (Argentina). She has published several books of poetry including *Versiones del paraíso/Variations on Paradise* (Del Dock, 2016) and *Temporada de invierno/Winter Season* (Bajo la luna, 2009, translation by **Allison A. deFreese**, forthcoming by Entre Ríos Books, Seattle, in late 2023). Her poems have previously been translated into French and have appeared in the anthology *Poésie récente d'Argentine, une anthologie possible/Recent Poetry from Argentina: a Possible Anthology*, published by Editorial Reflet de Lettres. A literary critic for *La Nación*, Argentina's leading daily paper, she is also the author of novels including *Un buen judío/A Good Jew* (Bajo la luna, 2016) and *La melancolía de los perros/The Sad Dogs* (Bajo la luna, 2020).

Marco Etheridge is a writer of prose, an occasional playwright, and a part-time poet. He lives and writes in Vienna, Austria. His work has been featured in more than seventy reviews and journals across Canada, Australia, the UK, and the USA. *U6 Stories: Vienna Underground Tales* is Marco's latest collection of short fiction. When he isn't crafting stories, Marco is a contributing editor and layout grunt for a new 'Zine called *Hotch Potch*.

Lawrence F. Farrar is a former American Foreign Service officer, with multiple postings in Japan, as well as assignments in Germany, Norway, and Washington, DC. Short term assignments took him to places as diverse as Beijing and Tehran, Caracas, and Muscat. Farrar's work has appeared in literary magazines more than 90 times. Many of his stories derive from events he experienced and people he encountered during 20 years living outside the United States. Farrar and his wife, Keiko, now live in Minnesota where he is a member of the Loft Literary Center.

Matthew James Friday is a British born writer and teacher. He has been published in numerous international journals, including, recently: *Acta Victoriana (CA)*, *The Oregon English Journal*, and *Shot Glass Journal*. The micro-chapbooks *All the Ways to Love*, *The Residents*, *Waters of Oregon*, and *The Words Unsaid* were published by the Origami Poems Project (USA). Matthew is a 2021 Pushcart Prize nominated poet.

A Pushcart and Best of the Net nominated poet, **E. Laura Golberg's** work has appeared in *Rattle*, *Poet Lore*, *Laurel Review*, *Birmingham Poetry Review*, *RHINO*, and the *Journal of Humanistic Mathematics*, among other venues. She won first place in the Washington, DC Commission on the Arts Larry Neal Poetry Competition.

David A. Goodrum is a writer/photographer, lives in Corvallis, OR. His poems are forthcoming or have been published in *Fireweed: Poetry of Oregon*, *Willawaw Journal*, *Spillway*, *Star 82 Review*, *The Write Launch*, and *The Louisville Review*, among others. Even before his early thirties, he was certain he would never write poetry again. He continues, it seems, to be wrong. About most things.

Benjamin Green is the author of eleven books including *The Sound of Fish Dreaming*. At the age of sixty-six he hopes his new work articulates a mature vision of the world and does so with some integrity. He resides in New Mexico.

Peter J. Grieco is a retired English professor and former school bus driver. His poems have been widely published in small magazines online and in print. His book length collections include *At the Musari-*

um, a series of semi-procedural verse based on word frequency lists, and *Misinterpretations of Dreams*, a series which interrogates Freud's seminal study of dream life. His chapbook collection of ekphrastic verse, *The Bind Man's Meal*, is forthcoming from Finishing Line Press.

Julia Hands is a writer and editor out of Seattle. She has fiction and poetry published or forthcoming from publications such as *Cream City Review*, *The Evansville Review*, *Whale Road Review*, *The Shore*, and *Aquifer: The Florida Review Online*.

Suzy Harris lives in Portland, OR. Her poems have most recently appeared in *Clackamas Literary Review*, *Fireweed*, *Poeming Pigeon*, and *Williwaw Journal*, among other journals and anthologies. She has been an Oregon Poetry Association prize winner, recently served as poetry editor of *Timberline Review*, and is the author of a chapbook called *Listening in the Dark*, a finalist in The Poetry Box's 2022 chapbook contest.

Michelle Hartman is the author of four poetry books, all available on Amazon & Barnes & Noble. Also, the author of 3 chapbooks, her work has been published in numerous journals as well as in various other countries. She is the former editor of *Red River Review* as well as the owner of Hungry Buzzard Press. Hartman holds a BS in Political Science-Pre Law from Texas Wesleyan University, and a Cert. in Paralegal Studies from Tarrant County Community College, who has named her a Distinguished Alumni.

Amanda Hawk lives in Seattle between the roaring planes and concrete jungle. She splits her time with her son and friends, and the city's neon lights. Recently, she has been published in *Volney Road Review*, *Drunk Monkeys Literary Journal*, *Anti-Heroin Chic*, *Eye to the Telescope*, and *the winnow* magazine.

Madronna Holden won the 2022 Kay Snow Poetry Award and was featured poet in *Camas Magazine's* 2022 "lore" issue. In her recent retirement from teaching, she has had the opportunity to focus on her poetry, which has appeared in over 30 literary journals, including *The Bitter Oleander*, *Verse Daily*, *Cold Mountain Review*, and *Valley Voices*—as well as three previous issues of the *Clackamas Literary Review*. She is the author of the chapbook, *Goddess of Glass Mountains* (Finishing Line Press 2021).

Tom C. Hunley has published poems in *California Quarterly*, *Catch Up*, *The Chaffin Journal*, *Chiron Review*, *Cimarron Review*, *The Comstock Review*, *Concho River Review*, *Connecticut Review*, *Crab Creek Review*, *Crab Orchard Review*, *Crazyhorse*, and *Curious Rooms*.

Casey Killingsworth has been published in numerous journals including *The American Journal of Poetry*, *Better Than Starbucks*, *The Moth*, and *3rd Wednesday*. His latest book is *A nest blew down* (Kelsay Books, 2021), and a new collection, *Freak show* (Fernwood Press), is due out in early 2023. Casey has a degree from Reed College.

Val Killpack is interested in how narrative, story, and myth can function as mediums for interrogation and apprehension in a complex, nuanced, and ever-changing world. He focuses on relationships of human to nonhuman—especially animals and environment—and the "becoming" which results. He is a PhD candidate in creative writing at Binghamton University in upstate New York. He has an MFA in writing and poetics from Naropa University's Jack Kerouc School of Disembodied Poetics and a BA in English literature from the University of Colorado at Boulder. He has taught writing at Binghamton University, Adams State University, Colorado Mountain College, and Breckenridge Creative Arts. Val has published in *Erasure*, *Caesura*, *Heavy Feather Review*, and elsewhere.

Greg Kosmicki is the author of 13 books and chapbooks of poems. *We Eat The Earth*, his newest collection, is due from WSC Press in November, 2022. He and his wife live in Alpine, CA.

Evan Litsios lives and writes in Vermont.

After a career in nonprofit health care, **Dennis Lum** now studies, reads, and writes poetry and serves as a volunteer with Legal Assistance for Seniors. He's currently working on a chapbook, *The Lingering*, which explores the experience of caregiving for loved ones. He is a husband, father, and grandfather living in Oakland, CA.

Nate Maxson is a writer and performance artist. The author of several collections of poetry, including *Maps To The Vanishing,* which is available now from Finishing Line Press. He lives in Albuquerque, NM.

Judith Mikesch McKenzie has traveled much of the world, but is always drawn to the Rocky Mountains as one place that feeds her soul. She loves change—new places, new people, new challenges—but writing is her home. Her poems have been published in *Wild Roof Journal*, *Bookends Review*, *Halcyone Literary Review*, *Plainsongs Magazine*, *Elevation Review*, *Scribblerus*, *Cathexis Northwest Press*, *Meat for Tea Valley Review*, and several others. She is a wee bit of an Irish curmudgeon, but her friends seem to like that about her.

Zackary Medlin grew up in South Carolina, ran away to Alaska, tried his luck in Utah, and now lives in Colorado, where he teaches creative writing at Fort Lewis College. He is the winner of the Nancy D. Hargrove Editor's Choice Prize, the Patricia Goedicke Prize in Poetry, and a recipient of an AWP Intro Journals Award. He holds an MFA from the University of Alaska Fairbanks and a Ph.D. from the University of Utah, where he was awarded a Clarence Snow Fellowship. His poetry has appeared in journals such as *Colorado Review*, *The Cincinnati Review*, *Grist*, and more.

Melissa Michal's work focuses on her community's histories and experiences. She is of Seneca, Welsh, and English descent and is a fiction and screenplay writer, essayist, photographer, and a DEI coach and Consultant. Melissa has work appearing in *The Florida Review*, *Arkana*, *Yellow Medicine Review*, *Transmotion*, *Presumed Incompetent the second edition*, and other spaces. Her short story collection, *Living Along the Borderlines* (2019), out with Feminist Press, was a finalist for the Louise Meriwether first book prize. She has drafted an adaptation of her story, "The Long Goodbye" from that collection. She has a novel and essay collection and is at work on a new dystopian novel.

Judith H. Montgomery's poems appear in *Bellingham Review*, *Rattle*, *Prairie Schooner*, and *Cave Wall*, among other journals, as well as in a number of anthologies. Her first collection, the chapbook *Passion*, received the 2000 Oregon Book Award for Poetry; the full-length *Red Jess* appeared in 2006; the chapbook *Pulse & Constellation* (2007) followed. Her second full-length book, *Litany for Wound and Bloom*, appeared in 2018 from Uttered Chaos Press; *Mercy*, which received the Wolf Ridge Press Narrative/Poetic Medicine Chapbook contest, appeared in 2019.

Cecil Morris, a retired high school English teacher, spends winters in California's Central Valley and summers on the central Oregon coast. His poems have appeared in *Cimarron Review*, *Ekphrastic Review*, *English Journal*, *Evening Street Review*, *New Verse News*, *Talking River Review*, and other literary magazines.

George Oliver has just finished a PhD on contemporary fiction at King's College London, where he also taught American literature for three years. He is both a short fiction and culture writer, and Assistant Editor at *Coastal Shelf*. His recent publications include *Avatar Review*, *Bruiser*, *Roi Fainéant Press*, and *Watershed Review*, and he was shortlisted for Ouen Press' 2019 Short Story Competition.

Ricardo Pau-Llosa is the 2023 featured poet in *The Birmingham Poetry Review's* 50th issue. His ninth collection of poems is due out in the fall 2023 from his longtime publisher, Carnegie Mellon University Press.

Violet Piper is a writer, musician, artist's assistant, camp director, and astrophysicist. She has published essays, stories, and poems in *Slate*, *Blue Mountain Review*, *Harpur Palate*, and others.

Vivienne Popperl lives in Portland, OR. Her poems have appeared in *Clackamas Literary Review*, *Timberline Review*, *Cirque*, *Willawaw*, *About Place Journal*, and other publications. She was a featured reader in the Oregon Jewish Voices 2022 program presented by the Oregon Jewish Museum and Center for Holocaust Education. Her first collection, *A Nest in the Heart*, was published by The Poetry Box in April, 2022.

David B. Prather is the author of *We Were Birds* (Main Street Rag Publishing, 2019), and his second collection, *Bending Light with Bare Hands*, will be published by Fernwood Press. His work has appeared in many publications, including *Prairie Schooner*, *Colorado Review*, *Cutleaf*, *Potomac Review*, *Sheila-Na-Gig,* and others. He studied acting at the National Shakespeare Conservatory, and he studied writing at Warren Wilson College.

Corey S. Pressman is a writer, artist, and teacher living in the Pacific Northwest. He has published poetry, academic chapters, and short stories. His artwork is represented by Portland's Blackfish Gallery. Corey is an instructor at the University of Portland.

Claudia Putnam lives in western Colorado with two huskies and a pissed-off cat. Her short memoir, *Double Negative*, won the Split/Lip Press CNF chapbook prize and came out in 2022. It was included in CLMP's 2022 nonfiction roundup. Her fiction appears in *Cimarron Review*, *phoebe*, *Confrontation*, *Variant Lit*, *Ghost Parachute*, and elsewhere. Overheard has nominated a piece for Best Small Fictions. A novella, *Seconds*, is available from Neutral Zones Press. Her debut poetry collection, *The Land of Stone and River*, appeared in 2022 from

Moon City Press. The George Bennett Fellowship from Phillips Exeter Academy is among her residency awards.

Bethany Reid grew up in southwest Washington state, but spent a few weeks every summer in Oregon camping and visiting her father's childhood haunts. She has four books of poetry, including *Sparrow*, which won the 2012 Gell Poetry Prize, and *Body My House* (2018).

Jacob Reina is a tutor an English student at Fresno State. His poems have been featured by *New York Quarterly, Watershed Review, Rougarou, Poets Choice, Allegory Ridge*, and *Cathexis Northwest Press*. Much of his work is deeply influenced by Persian and Russian literature.

Jim Richards' poems have been nominated for Best New Poets, two Pushcart Prizes, and have appeared recently in *Poetry Northwest, Copper Nickel, Hotel Amerika, Sugar House Review, Prairie Schooner, Salt Hill*, and others. He lives in eastern Idaho's Snake River valley and has received a fellowship from the Idaho Commission on the Arts.

Pier Roberts has been published in *The Spotlong Review, The Atlantic Unbound, The Adirondack Review, Travelers' Tales, Turkey: True Stories, Her Fork in the Road, A Woman's Passion for Travel: More True Stories from a Woman's World*, and *Escape Magazine*, among others. She participated in the Squaw Valley Community of Writers (2013) and received her Bachelor of Arts from UC Berkeley and her Masters in creative writing from Mills College. Pier is a teacher at an all-girls Catholic high school, where she teaches Great Books and Creative Writing. She lives with her teenage twins and two (possibly three) cats. Aside from reading and writing, Pier enjoys swimming and cooking.

Andrew Robin is a poet with a few books and chapbooks, most recently *Stray Birds* (Kelson Books) and *Small Pale Telegrams From The World* (Sixth Finch Books). Some recognitions include an Iowa Poetry Prize and a Distinguished Teaching Award from the University of Massachusetts Amherst. He lives with his wife Sarah on Lopez Island in the Salish Sea of Washington State, where he works as a registered nurse and volunteers as an EMT.

George Rose lives and writes in northern California, where he is the artistic director of a local youth theater company that produces plays written, directed, and performed by middle school students. His poetry has appeared previously in *Poetry Northwest*.

Laura Ruby has published numerous novels, including *Bone Gap* (HarperCollins, 2015) and *Thirteen Doorways, Wolves Behind Them All* (HarperCollins, 2019), both National Book Award Finalists. Her short fiction has appeared *The Florida Review*, *Pleiades*, and the *Beloit Fiction Journal*, among other magazines, and her poems are published or forthcoming in *Sugar House Review*, *Fantasy Magazine*, *Diode*, *The Dallas Review*, *Poetry South*, *The Nassau Review*, and *Bayou Magazine*. She teaches fiction writing at Hamline University and Queens University.

Birgit Lennertz Sarrimanolis has been published in *Cirque Journal*, *Five on the Fifth*, *Medicine and Meaning*, *Shark Reef*, and *49 Writers*. Her story "April Supermoon" aired on Juneau KTOO's Community Connections series. She was a finalist in the 2020 Pacific Northwest Writers Association literary contest and won second place in the 2021 Annual Writer's Digest Writing Competition. Her memoir *Transplanted* (Cirque Press Books) is available on Amazon. She regularly attends several writing conferences, including the Pacific Northwest Writers Conference, the Seattle Writing Workshop, and the Kachemak Bay Writers Conference. Birgit holds a BA in art history and German studies, an MA in art history, and a PhD in art education. She has lived in Indonesia, India, Chile, Argentina, Egypt, Germany, and Greece, but now calls Alaska home, where she writes overlooking the Tanana Valley.

Shawn Schenck is an author and musician from Portland, OR. His writing includes elements of the weird, fabulism, and horror. Shawn enjoys reading, watching movies, and spending time with his family. His favorite color is yellow.

Peter Serchuk's poems have appeared in a variety of journals including *Atlanta Review, New Letters, Boulevard, Booth, Denver Quarterly, New Plains Review*, and others. His latest book is *The Purpose of Things* (Regal House), a collection of short poems and photographs created in collaboration with photographer Pieter de Koninck.

Matthew J. Spireng's 2019 Sinclair Poetry Prize-winning book *Good Work* was published by Evening Street Press. An 11-time Pushcart Prize nominee, he is the author of two other full-length poetry books, *What Focus Is and Out of Body*, winner of the 2004 Bluestem Poetry Award, and five chapbooks, *Clear Cut*; *Young Farmer*; *Encounters*; *Inspiration Point*, winner of the 2000 Bright Hill Press Poetry Chapbook Competition; and *Just This*.

Don Edward Walicek lives in San Juan, Puerto Rico. His poetry has been published in *The Wild Word*, *New Feathers Anthology*, and *Califragile, A Literary Journal of Climate and Social Justice*, and *Chapter House*. He is a former Fulbright Scholar and fellow of the American Council of Learned Societies. His publications include the edited volume *Guantánamo and American Empire: The Humanities Respond*. A faculty member at the University of Puerto Rico's Río Piedras campus, he has served as editor of the Caribbean studies journal *Sargasso* since 2009.

A professor of English at Winona State University in Minnesota, **Myles Weber** has published work in the *Kenyon Review*, *the Southern Review*, *the Georgia Review*, *the Sewanee Review*, and many other journals. He is the author of *Consuming Silences: How We Read Authors Who Don't Publish* (U of Georgia Press).

Paul Willis has published seven collections of poetry, the most recent of which is *Somewhere to Follow* (Slant, 2021). Individual poems have appeared in *Poetry*, *Tahoma Literary Review*, and the *Best American Poetry* series. He is a recently retired professor of English.

The *Clackamas Literary Review* is typeset in Sabon LT Std, an old-style serif designed by Jan Tschichold, and in Optima, a humanistic sans-serif designed by Hermann Zapf, and printed on 50 lb. creme paper. Editing and design done by English Department students and faculty at Clackamas Community College, in Oregon City, Oregon.

Visit

CLR
CLACKAMAS LITERARY REVIEW

clackamasliteraryreview.org
clackamasliteraryreview.submittable.com
facebook.com/clackamasliteraryreview
@clackamaslitrev

Contact
clr@clackamas.edu

CLR

CLACKAMAS LITERARY REVIEW

the finest writing for the best readers

Clackamas Literary Review has been committed to publishing quality writing from around the world since 1997. Use the form below or visit us on Submittable to receive the latest and forthcoming issues.

Clackamas Literary Review

_____ 1 year $15

_____ 2 years $28

_____ 3 years $40

Name _____

Address _____

City / State / Zip _____

Email _____

Send this form and check or money order to:

Clackamas Literary Review
English Department
Clackamas Community College
19600 Molalla Avenue
Oregon City, Oregon 97045